Endof

"This book has a message for us: 'Your dreams matter and you are not alone.' It's a beautiful reminder that, while it takes courage, the story in our hearts can and must be pursued. So if you are ready for a partner on your journey to a life of hope and passion, *The Messenger* is for you."

—DOUG PAGITT, author of *Flipped*, pastor,
Goodness Conspirator, www.DougPagitt.com

"*The Messenger* is a simple tale that offers big hope to anyone willing to risk the climb."

—DONNA VANLIERE, *New York Times* bestselling
author of *The Christmas Shoes* and *The Good Dream*

"This world is starved for hope, and *The Messenger* is dripping with it, giving us a story we can all step into and find our place in. There is a positive energy coursing through this writing, and in a time when beauty and goodness seem difficult to find, this book helps us have eyes to see it."

—JOHN PAVLOVITZ, pastor, author,
and founder of The Table Ministry

"Mark and Cecil are fresh voices who provide life answers that stand the test of time."

—DAVE RAMSEY, nationally syndicated radio host
and *New York Times* best-selling author

"*The Messenger* a simple, yet emotionally complex tale of compassion and virtue. Set in a remote Scandinavian village of yesteryear, *The Messenger* tugs at each heart string it touches, taking the reader step by step through a broken father's ascent of a snow-capped mountain called life. With this novella, the authors create 'instant folklore' that begs to make its way into countless bedtime story moments."

—JEFFERSON MOORE, actor, writer,
and director at Kelly's Filmworks

"*The Messenger* offered a journey into my own heart, triggering reflection on all areas of life. Smeby and Kemp tell this story in a simple yet boldly direct way that caused me to stop and think on almost every page."

—MATTHEW CLARK, Chief Operating Officer
of Churchill Mortgage Corporation,
Brentwood, TN

"*The Messenger* is a fable about hope and discovering a life full of meaning. You will be challenged and inspired to climb whatever mountain is in front of you."

—JON GORDON, author of *The Carpenter* and *The Seed*

"Well-crafted, deceptively simple, and deeply wise *The Messenger* will be an encouragement to anyone who reads it. In a world that is too often self-centered and short-sighted, this book tells a story that we all can learn and grow from.

—THE REVEREND THOMAS MCKENZIE, Obl.S.B.,
pastor, Church of the Redeemer, Nashville, TN

"I loved this touching and inspiring story."

—NATE LARKIN, founder of the Samson Society
and author of *Samson and the Pirate Monks:
Calling Men to Authentic Brotherhood*

THE
MESSENGER

A JOURNEY INTO HOPE

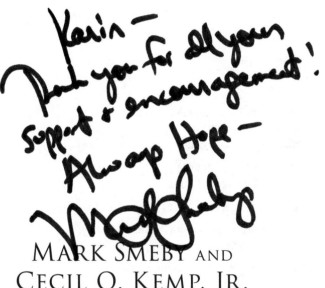

MARK SMEBY AND
CECIL O. KEMP, JR.

BroadStreet
PUBLISHING

Published by BroadStreet Publishing Group, LLC
Racine, Wisconsin, USA
BroadStreetPublishing.com

THE MESSENGER
A JOURNEY INTO HOPE

Published in association with the literary agency
WTA Services LLC, Franklin, Tennessee

ISBN: 978-1-4245-5038-8 (softcover)
ISBN: 978-1-4245-5039-5 (e-book)

Cover by Christos DeVaris and Chris Garborg
Typesetting by Katherine Lloyd at www.TheDESKonline.com

Printed in the United States of America
16 17 18 19 20 5 4 3 2 1

INTRODUCTION

W hat's holding you back from the life you truly desire? Maybe you'd say, "Well, I'm much too busy to go after my dreams. I have bills to pay and a family to take care of. I can't afford the luxury of living from my heart."

As gentle and graceful as we can possibly be, we'd like to suggest that you can't afford the cost of *not* living from your heart. We did that for way too many years—and grew tired of feeling like this world is a miserable place. But the problem wasn't outside of us. It was inside.

That's why we resonate so deeply with Robin Williams' character's plea to his boarding school students to carpe diem in *Dead Poet's Society*, or we cry when the pint-sized hero of *Rudy* gets to be a part of the final play of the last football game of his senior year at Notre Dame. These great movies echo within us the truth that life can be bigger, deeper, richer, sweeter, and more significant than the day-to-day grind seems to allow.

But this journey is going to take great courage—courage to wake up to the idea that there's got to be something more than just traveling the same tired ruts in the same roads—that there must be more to life than simply going through the motions day after day. So the next question is, "Now what?"

The next steps might feel like trying to scale a mountain rising in front of you—a giant, fear-imposing challenge that right now seems impossible. The more you consider this challenge, the easier it's going to be to justify sticking with the way things have always been—to avoid rocking the boat. And if you're anything like us, you can't help but wonder what other people will think about you if you step out of the ordinary and journey into the unknown in search of your own heart. You might look more than a little crazy. But you are not alone—we're in this together: this renegade band of men and women who are on a quest to look at life in a different way, setting aside our worries about what others might think, and choosing to live from the heart.

We can't wait to hear what this means for you. For Thomas, this journey leads him straight into the place where he is most afraid—a place that actually ends up holding the secret to the life he's been searching for. For us, as well as our protagonist, it means waking up to what kind of person we are, envisioning what kind of person we want to be, and continually aiming our arrows at that target—refusing to let the actions or attitudes of other people determine what our lives should look like.

This means waking up to the idea of being completely loved, regardless of how good or bad, strong or weak, faithful or fearful we are. It means learning how to give that love away to other people, regardless of how they treat us. And in the process, discovering how to live a life marked by hope, regardless of the circumstances.

This kind of hope is what we believe changes the world, lifts us up out of the ruts we've worn in our day-to-day lives, and carries us to places and into relationships we never could have imagined.

This is our hope for you.

Mark Smeby and
Cecil O. Kemp, Jr.

ONE

Bergland, a small village north of Oslo, Norway
1933

L ed through the snowy woods by the glow from the full moon, Thomas and Benjamin came to the edge of Lake Holderen and surveyed the frozen expanse. This was the secret place where the boys would go to get away from everyone—they would usually end up swimming or skipping rocks across the water during the other seasons of the year. But for now, they stood in wonder at the frosty stillness of the lake.

"Why don't we go out there?" Benjamin asked.

Thomas knew it was too early. Everyone in Bergland wanted to be out on the lake ice fishing, but it was hit-or-miss whether the ice was thick enough just yet. "Nah, I don't think that's smart. Look, we can see how thick the ice is here on the shore, but it's usually thinner the farther out you go. I don't think we should risk it."

"You're just like the rest of them, Thomas."

"What are you talking about?"

"You're just like everyone in Bergland. Afraid to take risks." Benjamin took his first steps, slowly moving out onto the ice. "You can't live your whole life on the shore, Thomas." He sounded frustrated with Thomas and Bergland and maybe the whole world.

"Well, in this situation, leaving the shore means I might become an ice cube." Thomas pulled his hat down further over his ears as a wicked chill made him shudder. The wind tore through his coat and sweater and stung his skin. "I'll just stay right here. Now, is that so wrong?" Thomas smiled at his friend. His smile made everyone feel comfortable the minute they met him, and it had stopped several fights before they ever started. He didn't want Benjamin to be angry with him. Not tonight.

"Maybe not for you, but for me it is." Benjamin became cockier with each step. Thomas watched as Benjamin stomped on the ice, just for effect, as if to scare Thomas. Benjamin paused and Thomas held his gaze for a moment. "You can stay safe on the shore," Benjamin called, "but I've got to find out what it's like out here on the ice! Maybe I'll see one of those hibernating fish!"

"You're crazy," Thomas laughed nervously, afraid for his daredevil friend. He was glad that Benjamin couldn't see his fear, or worse, the envy he felt. Thomas wished that he were an adventurous risk taker like Benjamin.

When Benjamin turned back around, Thomas took a tiny step off the shore onto the ice. It felt solid at first, but then he heard a crack and could see the telltale bubble underneath. He quickly stepped back. He wished his father were still alive and right here with them; his dad would tell him what to do.

But this just wasn't worth it, not even for a glimpse at a hibernating fish.

In eighth-grade science class, the boys had just been learning about the biological phenomenon of anomalous expansion. Thomas pictured a brown trout floating in suspended animation under the layer of ice: glassy eyes not moving, gills swelling ever so slightly to avoid detection of any sign of life, hovering between life and death. In order to survive the long Norwegian winter, the underwater species have the ability to lower their metabolic rate, reducing their need for food and oxygen. Activity slows to a minimum—sometimes giving the appearance that the animal may actually be dead. This underwater hibernation is designed to protect the species from the elements and predators seeking an easy meal in the cold, barren wilds. Once the weather warms and the ice melts, the higher temperatures resuscitate the fish, and life returns to normal.

"I think everyone in Bergland is anomalously expanding," Benjamin had whispered across the aisle to Thomas during their classroom discussion a few days before.

"You think they can be resuscitated?" Thomas whispered back, and Benjamin had smirked.

The brutal winters brought face-burning temperatures and coated the tree-lined lakes and streams with milky blue ice. All the inhabitants of the quaint mountain village seemed to shut down for months at a time. As the cold descended every fall, people sought the warmth, shelter, and battened-down isolation of their homes. Some never really seemed to fully return to life, even when spring came.

Benjamin and Thomas agreed that unlike fish, the people of Bergland stayed locked in their self-imposed hibernation, sustaining the lowest level of life possible to still be considered alive, though even that was questionable for a couple particularly comatose Berglanders.

Why was it so easy for people to live that way? The question baffled Thomas and Benjamin. But the other mystery was this: Why were they the only ones who thought that was a problem?

The boys liked to continue their analysis of Bergland in between classes.

"It's like they can't see any need to wake up. They are uncertain what existential dissonance they might encounter if they were to suddenly wake up and start living and breathing at the level for which they were created," Benjamin added, always a fan of using his ever-expanding vocabulary.

Thomas rolled his eyes. He couldn't even keep up with Benjamin's vocabulary. "I wonder if towns on the other side of the mountain are any different," Thomas said, pausing near the window in the hallway.

Both boys looked toward the horizon in silence for a moment. They had grown up hearing stories about this mountain, how the paths had unexpected twists and turns and deadly drop-offs. The mountain was said to be even more treacherous than the ice on the lake, and children were warned to stay away from it.

"We'll find out someday," Benjamin said. "Together."

Thomas nodded. It was easy to be brave; the mountain was far away.

That evening, Benjamin had told Thomas that he needed to get out of the house, and Thomas had agreed to join him at the lake.

Benjamin struggled with a paralyzing combination of his father's high expectations and his older sister's constant badgering him about being "dumb." That was always a mystery to Thomas. Didn't anyone in Benjamin's family listen to him?

But Lake Holderen was their place, the one refuge where Thomas and Benjamin could dream of moving somewhere far away from Bergland. Somewhere they could be whomever they wanted, without anyone telling them otherwise.

Now Thomas watched as Benjamin laid on the ice in the middle of the lake, flapping his arms and kicking his feet like a fish, gradually slowing his movement to imitate their hibernation instincts. Finally, Benjamin was still, his breath coming out in little white puffs of frozen air that hovered then disappeared into the night. Watching Benjamin lie still in the middle of the lake, Thomas felt the quiet ease of serenity. *If only I were braver*, Thomas thought, *I would be out there with him.* But Benjamin had been right about one thing: Thomas was just like most of the folks in Bergland. He just wasn't born for taking risks.

Benjamin stood then, cupped his gloved hands together, and yelled at the top of his lungs at Thomas. "It's awesome out here!"

Thomas waved his arms above his head in response.

Benjamin shouted, "Life's too short to live on the shore!"

Thomas heard the crack, the thunder of splitting ice that ricocheted off the mountain, instantly filling him with terror.

The ice that Benjamin had safely walked across only minutes before suddenly opened, and Thomas watched helplessly as the lake swallowed his friend without any excuse or justice. Paralyzed with fear, Thomas screamed, "Benjamin, NO!", but he realized there was no sound to his words. Everything inside of him cried out for help, but his body stood still and his voice was silent. Frozen in place, Thomas prayed for Benjamin to be able to save himself. He willed his friend to pop back up, grab the edge of the ice, and pull himself out.

But the ice settled and was still.

I'm supposed to save him, Thomas thought, *but I don't know how. I don't...* Panic rose in Thomas, making his chest tight and breathing difficult. He had heard what happened when people fell through the ice, how their wet clothes became an anchor, pulling them to the lake bottom, how the ice sealed itself and trapped its victim. Thomas imagined Benjamin watching the hole above him disappear, how the clothes meant to protect him were killing him now. Thomas was safe on the shore, but he had never felt so much fear. It was as if life had finally revealed itself to him. Nothing was safe, and there were no risks worth taking. The mountain loomed over him like a dark hole stretching across the night sky. Thomas knew the mountain was waiting to swallow him alive too.

In the years to come, Thomas would wonder again and again if he could have done anything to save his friend. But he also knew the world was frozen and treacherous. Even the tiniest crack in the ice could lead to a watery death, and those who survived the crossing would stand before the dreaded mountain.

There was no hope for anything better.

TWO

Thomas kept his memory of Benjamin alive by visiting the lake often in the following years, especially during the chilly winter months when he was feeling the most alone. Even two years later, he still felt Benjamin was waiting for him to act.

He had read that the frigid temperatures of Lake Holderen prevented submerged bodies from decomposing. Benjamin would have loved to talk about that. But the idea of it filled Thomas with sorrow. Benjamin would never be free, not even in death.

Thomas found himself dwelling on that fateful night many times throughout each school day. He had once been willing to help other students who weren't able to grasp difficult concepts, and that had earned him a good reputation. He had even loved jumping in when the teachers needed help with special projects.

But he was different after Benjamin's death. He wished he could be like his friend had been—a happy, optimistic adventurer—but he was weighed down by a strange grief, one greater than just the death of his friend. He couldn't figure it out or make it go away. He just wasn't willing to jump into a discussion or volunteer beyond what was expected of him. Something in his spirit had frozen and was submerged in an unreachable darkness.

Still, Thomas tried to not neglect his responsibilities. He met the expectations of his parents and teachers, and he resigned himself to a life he didn't understand or want.

But resigned was not a way Thomas ever imagined himself living. Before Benjamin's death he dreamt about places beyond the mountain; afterward he rarely lifted his eyes from the ground as he walked. He always planned to move away and chase after greener pastures and wide-open spaces.

But life continued to push and pull him along…and it didn't seem like many years had passed before Thomas had a wife, three kids, a job…and he hadn't moved more than one hundred yards from where he was born. He had all the responsibilities of a grown man, but he was still the frightened young boy stuck on the side of the lake. He had failed his best friend all those years ago, and Thomas couldn't help but worry that someday he might fail his own family. Especially Anna, his youngest daughter. Thomas desperately needed a miracle to save her, though he had never heard of one happening in Bergland.

People didn't talk about miracles. Not here.

THREE

Bergland
1953

The streets were empty and a peaceful silence had settled over the town on this Sunday morning. The sun was just beginning to peek through the trees on the east edge of the village, and Thomas knew people were waking up and slowly preparing for the day. The colorful flowers in the garden beds and windowsills were layered with fresh dew. Streams of smoke rose from chimneys around the perimeter of Main Street. The majority of the village's houses were positioned near this road, easing the villagers' walk to and from their local jobs. On the north edge of Main Street, Bergland's one-room schoolhouse was quiet for the weekend, primed for another week of classes that would begin the following day.

After an especially cold and snowy winter, spring had arrived with a gentle whisper, bringing with it new life. Thomas looked forward to the warmer temperatures and the opportunity to be outdoors, enjoying nature and all its hidden surprises. Each year he secretly wondered if this would be the season that would break the icy shell of Bergland's townsfolk, and his own melancholy. His lone moments of joy were found with his family, especially his three children: eight-year-old Andrew, six-year-old Erik, and four-year-old Anna, who had been sick with the polio virus for most of the past year.

But in the sleepy, silent village, there were no signs that this might be a year for miracles. Standing on his porch, Thomas watched as the sun spilled across the horizon in pink and gold. For a moment, he almost believed that something good might still happen here.

Then Thomas shook his head at the absurdity of the thought. His wife, Lena, was in the kitchen brewing coffee, and the rich scent made him restless to get on with the routine of the day. Nothing changed in Bergland. He ought to know that by now.

Even the children knew that. Nothing and no one changed. Children would always follow in the footsteps of their parents. The children of farmers would become farmers, the children of bankers would become bankers, and the daughter of the teacher would unquestionably be the next teacher for the village. Any amount of extra thought regarding their future would simply be a waste of time. Everyone knew what was expected of them and they complied. To question the established order was taken as a sign of pride. And in Bergland, there weren't many things worse than that.

This particular idea even had a name: *Janteloven*, or "The Law of Jante." Thomas remembered having to recite the principles in class years ago: No one should assume they're better than anyone else. No one should hope to be anything special. The law, which had existed for longer than even Thomas' teachers could remember, had been put into writing by Aksel Sandemose in his 1936 novel, *A Fugitive Crosses His Tracks*. The fictional town of Jante and its ten commandments fostered a hostile attitude toward individual success and individuality in general.

The law of Jante placed all emphasis on the collective population in order to aid in its survival and development. Jante was opposed to any one person achieving and standing out from the crowd. The principles had been handed down through the centuries in Bergland, and the town laws supported the ideal. Even the mayor had been elected solely to make sure the laws were never challenged. And since life in the village was peaceful, everyone seemed content—except Thomas.

That's why nothing ever changed in Bergland, and some referred to that as stability. Thomas saw it differently, but to challenge their way of life would imply an arrogance that wasn't acceptable. Even if change was sorely needed, and even if Thomas found the courage to speak out, he knew that life didn't always reward a risk.

Still, he knew Benjamin wouldn't want him to give up. Not now.

Anna had to be saved.

FOUR

I'm not prepared to say good-bye to Anna," Lena said as she slid Thomas the day's first cup of coffee. He noticed that her hand was trembling, perhaps because Anna was experiencing an unusually high fever this morning. Lena was terrified of losing Anna, and Thomas had never felt so helpless.

He would be taking the boys to church shortly while Lena stayed at home with Anna. They had explored all the medical options they could find and afford, but Bergland had limited options. Thomas knew that only God could save his daughter now, and he didn't have a lot of confidence that God would act. Thomas had watched bad things happen to good people for years now.

"How could anyone prepare for that?" he asked. Thomas thought of Benjamin and everything he wished he could've said to him. He reached across the table to touch his wife's hand, but she withdrew her hand and turned so Thomas couldn't see her face. She dabbed at her eyes with the edge of her apron.

"Maybe you could spend time with her today," Lena replied. She turned and straightened the place setting on the table, a look of concentration on her face. Routine had been her only salvation lately. Thomas knew she needed routine, order, and, above all, Lena needed to hold on to everything just as it was.

Thomas stopped himself from making an excuse, but he didn't know how to care for Anna, not like Lena did. He couldn't even explain how difficult it had been to know how to care for his sick daughter. Lena just always knew what was needed.

"You don't have to do anything special. Just be there next to her. She knows." Lena's eyes softened with compassion; she finally reached her hand to touch his.

"I...can do that. I can do that," Thomas replied. He leaned over and kissed Lena on the forehead, grateful for her sensitivity. As usual, she knew what he needed too. The thought gave him courage. "We're going to get through this," he said. "Anna's going to get better. I promise."

As Thomas made sure the boys were getting dressed in their Sunday best, he knew Pastor Sundquist was most likely unlocking the church doors and posting the morning's hymn numbers on the board at the front of the sanctuary. That was his routine, which Thomas suspected was just as sacred to the pastor as the book he taught from. Some pastors reviewed their notes or prayed, but the Bergland pastor wanted to make sure no one deviated from the program.

As Thomas arrived with his boys, the villagers were filing in quietly, just as they did every Sunday morning to make an appearance at church. An appearance meant sitting quietly for forty-five minutes in their usual seats, and, for the children, it meant doing their best to stay awake. Pastor Sundquist usually preached some version of what a horrible place hell was and why those who left the right path would find only despair. He'd pass the plate for an offering and then everyone would go home. The people of Bergland attended church religiously, although no one ever seemed worried about hell. Hell didn't have any place for the good people of Bergland, anyway. Their lives were too safe to arouse God's anger.

Thomas knew today would hold no surprises.

He sat quietly with his two boys, occasionally tapping the backs of their heads with his hand to wake them. Hell might have been an interesting topic for the youngsters to hear about, but anything gets boring after hearing it one hundred times. (427 times for Andrew and 356 for Erik, to be exact.)

Thomas didn't want to hear any more about hell, though, either. He had his own version of it, and it was more painful than anything Pastor Sundquist had ever described. Watching helplessly as Anna suffered and struggled for breath—that was a hell too cruel for words.

When Thomas had left this morning, Anna's bedsheets had been soaked with perspiration, yet she shivered as if she was freezing cold. The virus that had attacked her little body was a relentless, confusing enemy, and Thomas worried that anything he did would only make Anna worse. Lena kept a pan of cool water beside the bed and would wet a towel for Anna's forehead. This seemed to help relax her. Thomas prayed it was helping this morning.

Then he wondered if God even heard his prayers. He had prayed plenty of them since the nightmare began.

It had started as a sensitivity to touch. Anna had flinched when Lena's gentle fingers worked to braid her hair. Next came congestion, headaches, and stiffness in Anna's back and neck, then the dreaded paralysis of her left leg, and finally, her right. The doctors in Bergland thought the paralysis might eventually improve, but their main concern was Anna's decreasing ability to swallow or breathe. There was no hope for a girl who couldn't swallow or breathe.

Before her recent turn for the worse, Anna went everywhere with the family by using a wooden wheelchair made by the Swedish furniture company Gemla Möbler. Thomas was thankful for it and insisted that Anna join the family whenever they went out.

The villagers made an obvious effort not to stare or whisper when Anna was wheeled past them. They even refused to mention her illness, as if denying the problem would make it go away. Thomas had gritted his teeth many times to keep from yelling at someone. They had turned doing nothing into an art form, he thought. Or worse, a weapon. Their seeming indifference hurt him, and worse, it made Anna feel invisible.

Upon returning from church, Thomas could smell the delicious meal Lena had been preparing. The house had the aroma of a bakery. How she could care for Anna, manage household chores, and still cook mouthwatering meals was astounding to Thomas. The boys wanted to play outside, and Thomas waved them off to enjoy the sunshine.

After Lena shooed him out of the kitchen, Thomas took a deep breath for courage and walked to Anna's room. He couldn't stop the virus, he told himself…but the virus couldn't stop him from loving Anna, either.

He entered Anna's room and was surprised to find her sitting up in her bed, fully awake. A book was open in her lap.

"Daddy…" Her voice was soft and labored as she spoke on the exhale, but her smile was still radiant. Thomas waited for her to say more, but she didn't.

"Hello, honey." He sat in the chair next to her bed. "What are you reading?"

"A book…a princess…trapped…in a castle…an enemy… the prince rescues her."

"How does he do that?" Thomas asked.

Anna turned the pages of the colorful book, pointing to the drawings.

Thomas leaned over and turned his head to try and understand the story. "Let's see…the prince has to go through the scary forest…the trees talk to him…and they tell him he's not good enough. Then he has to climb up some big rocks…and he's never done that before, poor guy. Then he has to swim across a moat…filled with giant alligators." Thomas raised one eyebrow and Anna giggled softly.

"Well, it's better than snakes, I suppose," he continued. She turned the page for him. "And then he climbs up the side of the castle…and through the window to rescue the princess."

Anna smiled.

"After all that, she better be good-looking," Thomas said, making Anna giggle again. "His part in the story sounds scary."

"No. It's not," Anna answered. Her eyes seemed to communicate to Thomas that the story was more than just a story, at least to her.

"Why is it not scary?" Thomas asked. "Nasty trees. Big rocks. Alligators."

"The prince…is very brave."

"Well, then that's a great story, Anna. I love it. But I have another question for you."

"Yes?"

"What makes the prince so brave?"

"He loves…the princess."

"Not as much as I love you, my dear."

Anna beamed at his reply.

Thomas got down on one knee and kissed Anna's hand, as if he were the prince there to rescue her. Then he stood and hugged her. "Not as much as I love you," he said softly once more.

"I smell...pancakes," Anna said.

"You sure do. Let's go eat some before the boys eat them all." Anna smiled.

"Ooh, it smells...so good," she said as Thomas scooped her up. Carrying her into the kitchen, Thomas pretended to watch for alligators that might be waiting to gobble them both up. Anna loved it.

Today's post-church meal was a family favorite. Lena made pancakes thin as crêpes and smothered them with whipped cream and strawberry jam. A bowl full of fresh blueberries and a platter of crispy bacon were already on the table. The kids loved to roll up the pancakes and eat from one end to the other, usually with the jam dripping out the bottom end. Thomas and Lena kept the pancake flat and ate with a knife and fork. Thomas secretly wished he and Lena could eat like the kids and make a mess.

The family quickly devoured all the pancakes, berries, and bacon as if they hadn't eaten for weeks. Thomas could tell by the smile on Lena's face how proud it made her to create a meal they enjoyed so much.

He caught her gaze and held it. She smiled at him though he saw tears forming in her eyes. Lena had her gifts, and he had his, but none of them could save their daughter.

In the summer of Thomas' eighteenth year, Lena's family had moved to Bergland. Thomas immediately fell in love with the beautiful new girl and asked her to marry him on their first date. She waited until their third to accept.

"No sense in waiting when you've found your soul mate," Thomas told Jonathan, his one remaining friend from school. Since Lena hadn't grown up in Bergland, she was uncharacteristically warm and optimistic, especially compared to other people in town. Over the following fifteen years, the other ladies would try to counsel her on the principles of Janteloven, encouraging her to fall into step with the rest of them. She would smile and nod and then later vent to Thomas about how crazy they all were.

Lena had always wanted to live on a lake—with an exquisite kitchen and giant porch facing the water—so they built their dream house overlooking Lake Holderen. And after having two boys, they finally got the girl they had been praying for. The first fifteen years of their marriage seemed enchanted now that Thomas looked back on them, when their biggest arguments had been about baby names and nursery colors. Thomas had lost those fights, of course, and he hadn't really minded. He would give anything to go back in time now and trade his troubles.

Thomas shook himself back to the present moment. Was he doomed to always want to go back in time and repeat the past? Why did he feel so unprepared to face the future?

That evening, when Thomas was tucking Anna into bed, he looked his daughter deeply in the eyes and said, "We're going to get you up and walking before too long, okay?"

Anna revealed a toothy grin.

"And we are going to dance around the living room like we used to do." Thomas held back the tears forming in his eyes, hoping Anna wouldn't see.

"Daddy..." She breathed in and then out. "Don't be sad."

"Anna, I love you with everything in my body. You are the light of my life. I am not giving up. Just hang on a little longer, okay?"

Anna raised her finger and whispered something. It looked like she was trying to point to something outside. Thomas looked out the window at the mountain in the distance. Again,

Anna whispered the same unintelligible words, and then she began coughing.

"Lena!" Thomas called, but Lena didn't reply. She was getting the boys ready for baths and bed.

Thomas grabbed the plain linen cloth, wet it in the cool water on her bedside table, and placed it carefully on Anna's hot forehead.

"Don't say anything," he whispered. "Just sleep, okay?"

Lifting her head slightly, she tried to speak once more, but a cough shook her frail body. Thomas laid one hand on her chest, closing his eyes, and prayed with all his strength. "God help us."

And in the stillness that followed, he was convinced he heard little Anna whisper, "Climb the mountain."

FIVE

After tucking the children into bed, Thomas sat at the kitchen table, waiting for Lena to join him. She liked to have a few moments of her own before bed, washing up and brushing out her long hair.

Thomas looked down at his hands. He had strong hands, with thick veins and calluses on his fingers. Making a fist with his right hand, he wondered what he would do if forced to fight someone. Maybe it would be a relief.

People in Bergland didn't fight.

Like his peers, Thomas inherited his father's life. The blacksmith shop was handed down from his father, who had inherited it from his father. The men in the Hanson family had always been blacksmiths. It was the best job in the village, they said.

Of course, Thomas knew that every other kid heard that same line too. How could anyone know what the best job was? No one had ever tried anything different. He wondered what Benjamin would have done on the day he was to inherit his father's printing shop. Would time have broken Benjamin's spirit the same way it had broken Thomas'?

Thomas hung his head. Why had he stood idle on the side of the lake? *I can't just stand by and watch the same thing happen again.* How ironic, he thought, that when he was finally ready to leave the shore, ready to fight this unseen enemy that had dogged him all his life, there was no action to take. Saving Anna didn't require physical strength, courage, or will. All Thomas could offer her was his love, and that wasn't enough to save her.

Lena planted a kiss on the top of his head, startling him.

He reached up and rested one hand on his shoulder, and she patted it.

"Lost in your thoughts again?" she said.

"Lena," Thomas asked, "have you read Anna's book about the princess trapped in the castle on the mountain?"

"Don't think I have. When did you give it to her?"

"I thought you had gotten it for her."

Lena sat across from him, her face pink from scrubbing. Thomas thought she never looked more beautiful than at these moments, fresh faced and her hair loose and glistening.

"No, it wasn't me," she said.

Thomas shrugged. "Maybe one of the boys gave it to her."

"In that case, I hope it's not too scary."

"Anna wasn't scared by it. I think she loves it."

"I'll check it out."

"And Lena, she said something interesting to me. I think."

"What do you mean, you think?"

"Anna was having a difficult time breathing, and the coughing started again, but she pointed out her window toward the mountain. I thought I heard her say, 'Climb it.'"

Lena smiled with a sad twist to her lips. "She wants to climb the mountain?"

"No, I think she wants me to climb the mountain."

"No, Thomas, that's crazy. She's just trying to bring her story to life. All little girls want to be princesses."

"But Lena," Thomas asked delicately, "what if she feels like she's the one trapped in the castle…but the castle is her body…"

"Thomas…" Lena pushed away from the table. Thomas knew she felt as helpless as he did.

"Lena, what if she thinks there's something on the mountain that can help her?"

"Thomas, what could possibly be on the mountain that could help our little girl?"

"I don't know, but…"

"But, what?"

They sat in silence for a minute before Thomas confessed, "Lena, I've always been paralyzed by fear. I've stood frozen on the shore watching life happen. I can't stand here any longer. If there's something I can do to help Anna, I have to do it. Even if it's all in her imagination."

"But Thomas, all the doctors have examined her. We've done all we can. We just have to trust that she'll get better. Or…"

"Or what, Lena? Or what?"

Lena shrugged, unable to say the words.

"I can't do that, Lena. I'm sorry," Thomas replied, then stood up and walked out of the kitchen.

Lena called to him, "Where are you going?"

"I don't know." His hand was on the doorknob, and he turned back to look at her. "I really don't know."

Thomas walked aimlessly through the village for an hour, then decided to visit his closest friend, Jonathan. Thomas knew Jonathan would be up at this late hour, most likely reading a history book.

The porch light was on, so Thomas knocked on the smooth oak door and waited.

Moments later, Jonathan opened the door a few inches and peered out. "Thomas?" He opened the door wide and scanned the evening sky. "A fine night to be out for a walk."

"Do you mind if I come in?"

"Please do," Jonathan said, stepping aside. Thomas entered and followed Jonathan to the living room.

After Benjamin's death, Jonathan had been a lifeline for Thomas, the only boy at school who didn't ask a lot of questions about that horrible night. Like most friends, Thomas and Jonathan did not always agree, but they shared a wry sense of humor. Thomas appreciated Jonathan's patience, compassion, and loyalty. It also helped that their wives were good friends.

Sitting down on the couch, Jonathan closed his book and placed his glasses on top of it. "What's going on, Thomas?"

"Jonathan, do you ever just stop what you are doing and think, 'Why am I doing any of this?'" Thomas asked.

Jonathan frowned. Thomas guessed the question confused him, so he continued, trying to explain himself clearly. "Do you ever think that maybe there is something else out there besides the day-to-day routine? Our lives aren't bad, but don't you ever feel trapped? Don't you ever wish life could be more than this?"

"You sound exhausted," Jonathan said, his voice soft with compassion. "Are you feeling all right?"

Thomas sighed. Jonathan would have made a good father, but he and Brigitta weren't able to have children.

"No, I really don't think I am. But for the first time, I'm ready to fight it," Thomas replied. He stood and paced the room. "There has got to be a better way to live, more than just going through the motions—or living by Jante's law. That's not living at all. And worse, I think it might kill Anna. I can't just go through the motions, not if I want to save her."

Thomas knew that Jonathan was content with life being just the way it was. He had embraced the concept of living each day, doing what's expected of you, not thinking too highly of yourself, and not worrying much. It made Thomas jealous that life seemed to be so easy for him.

"Thomas, I wish I could help you, I really do. But I do know that I'm happiest when I'm doing what I need to do," Jonathan finally responded.

"But who tells you what you need to do? Is it this town? These rules handed down through the years?" Thomas asked, and then paused, reflecting for a moment. "Or is it fear telling us all what to do? Fear of what people might think? Fear of the unknown?"

"Thomas, is this really about Anna?"

"Jonathan, yes. I'm frustrated that I can't do anything to help her. I'm her father. I want her to get well. And I don't understand why she might not. All the doctors are just shaking their heads— even they don't know what else to do. I need more than the usual Bergland answers. There's got to be hope out there, somewhere, even when everything points to the contrary. It's certainly not here in Bergland."

Overwhelmed with emotion, Thomas rushed to the door and ran outside. Jonathan did not follow.

He stumbled over the curb at the end of the yard and fell flat on his face. Rising to his knees, he brushed himself off and shifted his gaze down the length of the road. He had never seen the view from this vantage point. It was amazing to Thomas how the tall trees along the street seemed to point toward the mountain sitting squarely at the end of the road, or what looked like the end of the road, if the road only had gone that far. The villagers stopped using that part of the road years ago, so, with lack of upkeep, the trees and undergrowth made an end to the road just past the house of the village treasurer. He remembered Anna pointing to the mountain through her window. But from this angle, the moonlight caused the peak to glow with an intensity Thomas had never before witnessed. He heard Jonathan's front door open. Turning, he saw Jonathan looking at him in concern.

"Are you going to be all right?" Jonathan asked.

Thomas looked back at the mountain. If he could climb to the top, the view would offer a new perspective on the village below.

"I don't know," Thomas replied.

SIX

After work the following day, Thomas walked into the kitchen as Lena was cooking the evening's meal.

"Oh man, it smells so good in this house. How did I end up marrying a world-class chef?"

"Thomas…flattery will get you everywhere."

"Oh will it now?" He snuggled up to her and kissed her neck.

"Maybe. But right now I have to finish this gravy. Would you pull the bread out?" She glanced over at the oven.

Thomas looked around the kitchen and grabbed the oven mitt. "What are you making?"

"The special tonight is minced beef, rolled into balls and fried, with gravy on top. Peas and boiled potatoes added just for fun."

"Sounds amazing. I am a lucky man. We are a lucky family."

"The bread, dear," she said, glancing again at the oven.

"Yes, the bread." Thomas opened the oven and took out the fresh loaf. "Can I ask you a question?"

"As long as you don't mind me pretending to listen while I work," Lena smiled.

Thomas set the bread on the counter to cool. "This is going to sound really crazy. I can't stop thinking about the mountain. I think I'm supposed to climb it. For Anna's sake."

Lena set down the spoon she was using to stir the gravy. "How is climbing the mountain going to help Anna?"

Thomas shrugged. "I don't know, but I have to find out. Just because I don't know the answer doesn't mean I can't ask the question. Does that make any sense? I know I sound crazy."

"First of all, yes, you do sound crazy. Secondly, I love you. And I trust you. So if this is something you need to do—I can't believe I'm saying this—but you should do it."

Thomas exhaled in relief. He hadn't realized he was holding his breath until now.

"Even if you were the worst cook in Bergland, I'd still be the luckiest man in town." He leaned over and kissed Lena on the cheek. She rested her hands on her hips.

"Yes, you would. Now round up the kids for dinner."

Thomas had stood outside his blacksmith shop several times throughout the day to stare at the mountain.

It was rumored that the mountain swallowed anybody who ventured up its rough stone trails. Because of stories about ancestors who lost their lives while climbing, the mountain stood as a gigantic monument to the danger attached to any risk taking. The villagers resented the cold shadows it cast across the village and the way its hulking form blocked their view of the sunset.

Now Thomas wondered if the beautiful, snow-capped peak and elevated ridges pointed to the heavens, to entice him to reach for higher and greater things. Everyone else dismissed the commanding offer from above, but Thomas wanted what no one else had, so it was time to do what no one else would do.

Thomas cleaned up the kitchen while Lena got Anna ready for bed. The boys were busy washing up, and so Thomas finished the kitchen and settled into his favorite overstuffed chair in the living room, directly across from Lena's.

They liked to joke that getting into the chairs was always easy, but the older they got, the harder it was to get back out.

Lena joined him a few minutes later and opened the novel she'd been reading, then closed her book and looked at Thomas. "I've been thinking about what you told me. I know I said that you should do it, but I'm having second thoughts."

Thomas was surprised. Lena didn't often have second thoughts about anything. "What do you mean?"

"The mountain scares people. I know it's absurd what they say and that the stories are just rumors. But it might really be dangerous, maybe in ways we don't understand. Could there be even a smidgeon of truth to the stories?"

"Lena, we can't let fear have any place in our lives."

"Thomas," she interrupted. "That's just it. I want to hang on to what we have. I don't want anything to happen to you...to us."

"Oh, honey." He stood and, kneeling at the side of her chair, took her hand in his. "It's all going to be okay. Anna is going to be okay. I'm going to be okay."

"Someone will see you and then the gossip will start. You might lose business, and we still have medical bills to pay."

"If somebody judges me for trying to help my daughter, then I don't want their business anyway."

"But climbing the mountain just because Anna told you to? People will call you crazy."

"I've been called worse." He smiled at Lena, but she didn't return it. "I can't control what people think about me or how they respond to what I do. But please, Lena, I have to do this."

Lena pulled her hand from his. Standing, she walked silently into the kitchen.

SEVEN

Lena had spent nearly an hour that evening preparing a back-pack for him. She put things in, then took them out, and finally settled on a jar of water, leftovers from the night's meal, and matches. Thomas added a knife, a handful of leaves from his yard, and a picture of his family.

Later in bed, he tried in vain to sleep. He tried whispering a few words of prayer, but they seemed as futile as ever. After all, God only watched as Anna grew sicker every day. Thomas had gone to church his whole life and knew all the books of the Bible, but apparently God wasn't impressed.

Religion was just another way the village killed dreams with rigid rules and structure. Thomas could not forget all the times he had heard how God is ultimately in control of everything that happens, and in Thomas' experience, most of what happens here on earth is bad. Didn't that place some sort of culpability on the Divine?

Thomas stared at the ceiling until a distant light began to

illuminate the sky. Finally, hoping there would be answers ahead, Thomas set off into the unknown.

Reaching the base of the mountain within the hour, he took one last look back and set his foot onto the path.

The first thing that surprised him was that the villagers had been at least partially right: the path was overgrown with thick vines and thorny branches, and the ground was covered with sharp rocks. If Thomas slipped or strayed from the path, he would bleed. Watching carefully where he put each foot, he climbed higher, pink and gold rays from the sun gaining on him from the east.

After another hour, exhausted from the terrain and exertion, Thomas stumbled onto a small clearing. Grateful, he decided to sit down and rest, and he briefly closed his eyes.

He was awakened with a startle; something in the brush had made a sudden movement.

"Probably just a squirrel," Thomas told himself. The glow of dawn had emerged in the distance—the sun not directly visible, holding itself below the horizon, but scattering sunlight into the atmosphere.

Rubbing his eyes, he reached for his bag to silence the growl in his stomach. The temperature was considerably lower than he had anticipated, and he shivered, rubbing his arms to keep warm.

Thomas decided he was, indeed, crazy. This mountain was never meant to be climbed.

After a bite of food, he decided to turn back.

Standing, he glanced around the clearing, looking for the path, hoping to retrace his wayward steps. There was no sign of a path. His head started to pound. "Don't panic," he told himself.

Then he heard a voice—someone having a quiet conversation not too far from him. He turned to face its direction, but a thick green shrub blocked it. If he got scratched up it would upset Lena, but that was preferable to not making it home at all.

He burrowed through the shrub, letting the branches tear at his clothes, shielding his face with one hand.

"And God, I pray that you will continue to accomplish your will in my life. Your will, not mine. Bring me the one you desire for me to meet and keep me from those who—" the voice stopped.

Thomas saw what looked like an elderly woman in a crouched position, arms outstretched and palms open to the sky. Her long grey hair was pulled back into a bun, and her clothes were loose and colorful. She looked like she could've been a gypsy or an art teacher.

She took a breath and continued, "—and keep me from those who would do me evil. Amen," she finished. She sat silently.

The quiet fell heavy on Thomas while he waited to see her next move. The woman sat halfway up, still on her knees, hands on her legs. He could see more clearly how frail she was, though her wrinkled face had a peace about it. It was as if her spirit was bigger than her body. Without as much as a glance, she whispered, "I have been waiting for you." She waited another moment, then turned and looked directly at Thomas.

His fear slipped away. Warmth filled his entire body as he looked into her clear blue eyes. "For me? Waiting for me?" he cautiously asked, stepping closer to her.

"Today is the day for which you have been preparing your entire life," she said, with a grace and confidence that Thomas had never heard. It was as if each word was a delicate musical note.

He couldn't speak and he stood as still as a tree. Then he felt the blood circulating through his body at an increasingly rapid pace, like his heart was creeping up into his throat. He tried to swallow; his hands began to shake.

She continued, "God wants to use you to awaken the slumbering souls around you."

"Me?" Maybe she was mistaken. "But why..." he began to ask the woman.

She interrupted, "Because you chose to climb the mountain. God has promised that whoever would dare to climb the mountain would be met with help from above. That is where I come in."

He suddenly realized she was mistaken. "I'm not sure you have the right person. I'm here to see if there is something on this mountain that will help my sick daughter."

The woman smiled knowingly. "I have all kinds of gifts to give you that will enable you to accomplish your task," she replied in a gentle tone of voice.

"I'm sorry, but are you saying you can help my daughter?"

"The gifts on the mountain are for you, so that you'll be able to help your daughter and anyone else who needs it."

"Who are you, exactly?" Thomas was confused. Did this mysterious woman have a supernatural gift of insight?

"You ask my name? My name is Sophia. I will tell you more about myself over time. But first, it is time to get to know yourself," she replied.

Thomas noticed the sun had now risen over the village, casting long morning shadows across the town. The view from this spot on the mountain allowed him to see things he had never noticed before. He saw his own house. His backyard looked smaller than he thought it was, and the neighbors' houses on either side were so much larger than his own. *Are these the new perspectives I'm supposed to see?* Thomas wondered. There wasn't anything significant about the houses.

"You are going to see many things you have never seen before—new ideas, new perspectives—if only you are willing to learn and grow." The old woman spoke gently, taking a step toward Thomas and reaching out her weathered, bony hand.

Thomas took a step back. Had she heard what he was thinking?

His hand rose toward the old woman's, seemingly beyond his control. Their fingers touched and Thomas felt as if he was connected to the source of life. He closed his eyes as they stood still, hands locked.

Then he realized that he was still stuck on the mountain with no way back down.

"When you need to know the way up and down the mountain," she whispered, "ask the One who made it."

EIGHT

Thomas looked around where they stood, relieved to see the path at the far edge of the clearing. He guessed the people who used to climb the mountain would have used this point on the path to rest and sometimes even spend the night. There was a beautiful view of the countryside below, enough open space to see the stars above, and a slight, rocky overhang that would protect travelers from the elements.

The birds began their early morning chirping, flying over Thomas and the old woman as if they were supervising their activities. "Let's figure out what kind of person you want to be," Sophia said, as if she had done this her whole life.

"But what about my daughter, Anna? You said you could help her."

"Thomas, you are going to have to trust me. Yes, I will help your daughter, but first we need to focus on you."

"None of this makes any sense to me right now, but I'm willing to do anything to help Anna. Anything."

"You have decided to go on a journey up this mountain. But the journey I want to take you on is a different mountain. It lives inside you." Sophia gave him a toothy grin.

Thomas let out a nervous laugh. "So, I have to figure out who I want to be...and that's the mountain?"

Sophia nodded. "That's a part of the mountain, yes."

"What are the other parts of the mountain?" Thomas asked.

"We will get to that. But first, let's figure you out. We'll keep the good stuff and get rid of the bad stuff."

"Do I get final say in what stays or goes?"

"Funny you should ask," she answered with a gleam in her eye. "There are things you are going to try to hold on to for the rest of your life—things you already know you need to let go of. But I will tell you a secret..."

Thomas leaned in closer to her. She smelled faintly of rosemary and lemons.

"The secret is found in letting go," Sophia said. "Release whatever you think you need to hold on to. And trust that the benefit of letting go will be greater than the security of holding on. In letting go, you find the deepest satisfaction. The deepest hope."

Thomas found her words difficult to believe. "Hope? For what? As in, I hope that Anna will get better? I already have that kind of hope."

"That is desire, not hope. And we all desire something," she smiled. "But now it is time for you to discover what is the very best thing to desire in this life."

He suddenly pictured the pile of work he had at the shop and realized that he should be down in the village taking care of business. He was much too busy to spend any more time talking to this strange woman. He didn't need a stranger pointing out his faults.

He cleared his throat. "That sounds like a good way to look at it. Give me a list of things I can do to get this all taken care of. Then you can heal Anna and everything will get back to normal."

"Hmm," Sophia shook her head. "Unfortunately, we're talking about major work that needs to be done here."

Thomas raised his eyebrows, offended by her bluntness, but secretly he suspected she was right.

"This is not about giving you a list of things to do," she replied.

"Go on."

"This is your first assignment," Sophia said. "On our journey of trying to figure out the person you want to be, the person that this world needs, I would like you to ask everyone what they think about you."

"That's ridiculous. I can't ask people that." Thomas ran this idea through his head and pictured everyone laughing at him. The people in Bergland would never talk to each other in such a manner. It certainly wouldn't fit within the parameters of Janteloven.

"As long as you want to learn, I will be here to help you." Sophia took a step back. "But before you can learn, you must first learn to trust."

Thomas was silent.

"Will you come back tomorrow at sunrise, and each day after?" she asked. "Will you come back until you have found what you are looking for?"

"You really believe this is where I will find what I need?" he questioned the old woman and looked around this strange mountain sanctuary. "And you promise all this talking will lead to you helping my daughter?"

"This is my secret place," she explained. "It has been for several decades now. I come here each day to connect with God—to tell him everything. All he asks is that I come seeking him. He always meets me. One day soon, you will find your own secret place. Until then, I will be here and so will he," she ended, pointing toward the peak of the mountain.

She turned and slowly walked away from Thomas, heading down through a pathway cleared in the brush. He heard her start to sing, and he listened as she got farther and farther away until all he could hear was his heart pounding in his chest. He swallowed hard and began the climb down the mountain. The path was still rocky, and the vines still scratched and tore at his clothes, but he didn't mind. This was the path that might lead him to all the answers.

NINE

Every couple hundred paces he would stop, shake his head, and mutter to himself. It must have been a dream, Thomas decided.

"I have got to stop working such long hours."

"I might have touched some poisonous plant."

He made every excuse to rid himself of any responsibility to follow through on Sophia's assignment. Still, something in his heart told him he was only trying to avoid the truth. "But this isn't about me; it's about Anna. I have to remember that."

As he approached the village, he started hearing the sounds of the new workday. The familiar sounds were a relief to Thomas. If he could only get settled into his routine at the shop, surely his frazzled mind would return to a normal state. But first, he wanted to stop and tell Lena what happened.

"Lena?" Thomas called out, walking in the front door of their house. She walked out from the kitchen, wiping her hands on her apron.

"Seriously, what are you cooking now? It smells like heaven in here."

She kissed him and asked, "What happened on the mountain?"

"Oh Lena, you're going to think I'm completely crazy."

"We already agreed on that," she reminded him.

"But I met someone up there, and I believe she can help me, help us…help Anna."

"What? She? What is she, a doctor? A miracle worker?"

"No," he answered with a laugh. "Sophia is the sweetest little old woman you will ever meet. Turns out she's been waiting for someone from Bergland to climb the mountain so she can begin mentoring them."

"Waiting? Mentoring? About what?"

"I'm not sure exactly, but she said that she can help Anna. I'm willing to do anything she says."

"Anything?" Lena raised her eyebrows.

"Lena, she's an old woman. Very old. My love, you have nothing to worry about."

"Okay, I trust you." She hugged him.

"I will tell you more later. I have got to get to work."

"And I have a cake to bake." She smiled and walked back toward the kitchen.

"I love you, Lena. And your delicious cakes."

Laughter rang throughout their house.

Before he left, Thomas went into Anna's room and kissed her on the forehead. "Love you, princess…"

"Love you…Daddy."

Thomas noticed the book about the princess and the mountain resting on Anna's bedside table. He pointed to it. "Anna, your mother and I were wondering…where did you get that book?"

Anna glanced at the book and a soft smile spread across her face. "Sophia."

Thomas froze. It wasn't fear he felt, but the strange cold shock of realizing he was in the middle of some divine encounter.

"Sophia?" he asked. "How do you know Sophia?"

Anna inhaled deeply before speaking. "When I…was in the hospital."

"She was a nurse?" Thomas asked.

Anna shook her head no. "She read…to the children. At night. When they were…scared."

Goosebumps crept along Thomas' arms. "And she gave you the book?"

Anna nodded, her hair falling over her eyes. Thomas gently pushed her hair back behind her ear and tapped her nose, making her smile again. "Get some rest," he said, and left for his shop.

Throughout the extremely busy day, his lack of concentration kept distracting him from his work. He was unable to shake the story Anna had told him and the words Sophia had said to him: "God wants to use you to awaken the slumbering souls around you." *How could all this relate to Anna getting well?* he wondered.

Settling into bed next to Lena that night, he told her what Anna had said and about how Sophia said that they had to work on him first, and then she could help Anna.

"Sounds like this mountain visit is more about you than Anna," Lena said.

"I know. And it makes me uncomfortable."

"What does she think you need to work on?" she wondered.

"I have no idea. Maybe it's something about my job…me needing to work less or something like that."

"So, are you going to see her again?" Lena yawned. Taking care of Anna was becoming harder every week. They were nearly out of money, and Lena was nearly out of strength.

"Yes, she wants me to keep coming back. And I'll keep going back until we get Anna all better."

"I don't really understand, and sorry I'm so tired. But if it's going to help Anna, then it sounds like our last hope." Lena yawned, turned over, and dozed off.

Staring at the ceiling, Thomas lifted up a silent prayer. "God, I am not sure what you are up to, if indeed you are involved in this. But I need you to heal my daughter. I am certainly open to awakening the slumbering souls around me if that is what you want me to do. But if I am actually crazy and I only imagined this old woman, help me figure that out too." He fell asleep before he could say, "Amen."

While he slept, Thomas again climbed the mountain in a dream, only this time he was surrounded by dozens of other people who were desperately trying to climb as well. The other climbers kept asking Thomas if he knew a shortcut to the top of the mountain. His mouth was unable to form any words. He wanted to tell them that there was no shortcut—that you actually have to climb the whole mountain to get to the top. He helplessly watched as the other people made turns off the main trail, wandering into overgrown weeds and even off the steep, rocky edges of the mountain.

The number of climbers slowly dwindled down to two, Thomas and one other man whose face he did not recognize. The grief and heaviness Thomas was bearing watching the other climbers fall off the path made him feel like he had a backpack filled with stones he was trying to carry up the mountain. Thomas looked at the other man and tried to communicate with an expression. "You are the next one to go," Thomas tried to say, "and I really do not think I can bear to see one more person miss out on what is ahead."

He heard Sophia's singing. Thomas tried to call out, "Sophia! Help us!" But still no sound came out of his mouth. "Sophia!" He fell down on his knees, but instead of landing on the path, he continued falling as if he had stumbled into an endless black pit. Arms and legs flailing, he cried one last time. "Sophia—"

Thomas immediately sat up straight in his bed, sweat covering his body, his breathing heavy. Lena mumbled, "Another bad dream, Thomas? You really should…" She was asleep again before she finished.

A stream of moonlight had broken through the window beside their bed. Thomas looked down at the palms of his shaking, sweating hands and then at their backs. A tree branch rubbed up against the window with a scratch and then a tap. Another tap, then a scratch. Pause. Then two taps. *It's a signal of some kind*, Thomas thought. Then the music began again, the same singing as in his dream. There was no question it was Sophia and that she must be near.

He jumped out of bed, grabbed a coat, and pulled his boots on over his socks. Running out the door, he immediately began whispering loudly, "Sophia! Where are you? Sophia?" He ran all around the house to the bedroom window, hoping to find some sign of the old woman.

Thomas stood silent in the moonlight. A faint echo of Sophia's singing drifted on the breeze coming from the direction of the mountain. He turned and looked at the mountain. Again, its peak glowed.

"What sort of answered prayer is this?" Thomas shook his head, confused and exhausted. The only way Thomas could prove to himself that he had not gone completely mad would be to climb the mountain the next morning. If he went up the mountain and didn't find the meeting place or the old woman, he would know it was just a dream.

He hoped Sophia was real. He needed to believe that there was still time to ask for a miracle.

For everyone.

TEN

Lena…" Thomas whispered to his still sleeping wife.

"Oh, Thomas…what time is it?"

"You don't have to get up yet. It's still early, but I have to go."

"Then go. You don't have to ask my permission." She rolled away from him and pulled the blanket up higher around her shoulders.

"No, I mean up on the mountain."

"Oh, I thought you meant…"

"I had a horrible dream. And I'm scared that Sophia was a dream too. I've got to find out."

"I love you, honey. Go."

Thomas kissed her on the cheek and rose to get dressed for the hike.

This time, the journey was easier for Thomas since he had a better idea of what to expect from the path. The rough terrain was no surprise.

The shrubbery he walked through began to look more familiar until at last he knew he was near. He saw the rocky overhang ahead and exhaled in relief. The chirping of the birds called him to keep walking in their direction. He cautiously looked between the branches of the trees and shrubs, hoping to catch a glimpse of Sophia. He could not see anything until he came to the last bush before the path opened wide onto the little meeting place. Everything was exactly how he remembered it, except there was no sign of the old woman.

Thomas called out, "Sophia? Are you here?" He noticed the sun was about to peek out over the horizon just beyond the village below. The birds sang their approval for this new day of sunshine.

When there was no answer, his heart sank as he thought about Anna. Sophia was their last hope. If she had been a dream, a product of his imagination, then hope was no more than that too.

"I can't do this alone," he whispered.

"Yes, thank you, God!" he heard Sophia's voice cry out.

Thomas turned. Sophia walked toward him with her frail arms raised.

"I'm here. And I knew I would see you again," Sophia said. He was stunned, even more than by their initial meeting. The whole thing...she was real—it hadn't been a dream. This was really happening.

"How did you know I would be here?" he asked. "I didn't decide until this morning."

"Thomas, there is no other path left for you," she answered with compassion. "You cannot go back to the way you have lived. You wondered if there is something more, and now you know. There is something more. An incredible gift has already been given to you. What you choose to do with it now is your gift back." Sophia's eyes crinkled at the edges.

He looked down into the village and, seeing his house, thought about Lena and their three children. They seemed like quite a gift.

"It is more than your family, Thomas," Sophia continued. "They will bring you joy and love like you have never imagined, but there is still something deeper to find."

"You understand this is pretty strange," Thomas said. "I spent most of yesterday thinking I was going completely crazy—hoping you were real, that we can save Anna, but preparing myself to find out that you weren't."

"I will try not to take that personally," she chuckled.

"No, of course not," he answered as he lifted his head to watch a bird fly overhead. "But what about the dream I had last night?"

"How did you feel in the dream?" Sophia asked.

"How did I feel?"

"Yes."

"Why do you always ask such difficult questions?" Thomas asked. Sophia smiled but remained silent.

"I felt helpless," Thomas said finally. "I was climbing the mountain with a whole bunch of other people. And one by one I saw them disappear. As I saw each climber falling off the path, the load I was carrying got heavier and heavier. I was getting angry...mad...frustrated, even, that the choices other people were making were going to hurt them."

"Perfect," Sophia said.

Thomas raised his eyebrows.

"That frustration, that sensitivity to the harm that can come from the choices people make, will carry you a long way," Sophia said. "So, how is your first assignment coming along? Did you ask anybody what they thought about you?"

Thomas had been afraid she would ask this question. "It's only been a day, and a crazy one, at that," he answered.

"How about tomorrow morning, then?"

"And this is all going to lead to a miracle for Anna?"

"I promise," Sophia replied.

"All right," Thomas said. "I will meet you here tomorrow at sunrise."

"That's my boy," Sophia said.

Your boy? Thomas thought as Sophia turned and walked down the path to the other side of the mountain. He heard her begin to sing, just as she had done in his dream.

He wondered now how much of his life had been nothing but a dream, and if he was only now waking up.

Eleven

Thomas walked quickly, each step light and easy. He knew something was already changing inside of him, opening, like shutters slowly opening on a battened-down house. Or like the top layer of ice gradually melting on a frozen lake. He was beginning to see things he never knew were there before, even seeing things about himself.

Thomas walked the familiar path to work, but this time he noticed how the tree branches hung over the path beyond the post office, as if their limbs were locked in an embrace. He smiled to himself as he remembered how his hand embraced Sophia's wrinkled one.

Have I been wrong this entire time? he wondered as he walked through the streets toward his shop, seeing people looking at him, smiling, extending their morning greetings. As he arrived at the door to his shop and put his hand on the knob to open it, he noticed the detailed carvings that covered the door. He closed his eyes and tried to remember if the door was new or if he had only forgotten how beautiful it was.

He caught himself simply going through the motions in his shop, especially as he assisted customers. Thomas had always avoided eye contact with people, focusing on their request instead. But today, as each customer left the shop, Thomas had a gnawing feeling that he had missed something—a feeling that he should have taken an interest in them beyond just what size of nail they requested.

Thomas decided to attempt Sophia's assignment.

"Good morning! Good to see you!" he said as Isaac, one of the village farmers, entered his shop. Isaac looked at Thomas with half-squinted eyes, appearing to question Thomas' motives for being so friendly. "What can I do for you today?" Thomas continued.

"I need a new pot," Isaac said. "One that can hold a lot of meat and vegetables."

"Oh, is this for your wife?" Thomas asked.

Isaac looked at Thomas, his eyes opening wider. "Why…yes, it is." He almost broke into a smile.

"Great," Thomas replied. "I know a design she would love. I can have it for you by tomorrow, midmorning. Is that all right?"

"That would be great." Isaac turned to walk out when Thomas stopped him.

"I'm sorry, but could I just bother you with one more question?"

Isaac looked left and right. "Okay," he said.

"What reputation do I have here in the village?" Thomas asked, the sweat on his brow beginning to form. "What do people say about me behind my back?"

Isaac cleared his throat nervously. "Thomas. People say that…this is tough. I mean, you're real great and all. People say you are..." There was an uncomfortable pause, as if Isaac was holding his breath, right up until he finally thought of the right word. "Nice." He quickly turned and reached for the door.

"Thanks, Isaac," Thomas called. "Have a great day. And see you tomorrow!" As the door closed behind Isaac, Thomas was sure he had pushed too far. He let out a growl of frustration.

"I am...nice?" Thomas said out loud. "That's it? I've lived in Bergland my whole life and all people can say about me is that I'm nice?" He slammed a hammer against the table in front of him.

Thomas knew he had a problem. Sure, he was not a criminal or a drunk, reputations that might be more difficult to amend. But...nice?

A few minutes later, the shop door opened and in walked Jonathan, a welcome sight to Thomas.

"Jonathan, I am so glad to see you," Thomas said.

Jonathan scratched his head. "Really?"

"I sure am."

"What's the occasion?" Jonathan inquired.

"No occasion. It's just...Jonathan," Thomas said. "Do you think I am nice?"

"Of course you're nice, Thomas," Jonathan answered, his brow wrinkled in bewilderment.

"No, I don't mean, do you think I'm a nice person, but do you think that's all that I am? Nice, and that's all?" Maybe Anna's illness was his fault. If he hadn't been so "nice," maybe he would have found a cure by now.

"Is this one of your 'there's got to be something more to this life' questions?"

"No, I already know there is something more." Thomas sighed. "I know this is going to sound strange, but I think that figuring out the person I'm supposed to be is somehow tied into Anna getting better."

"What is that even supposed to mean?"

Thomas wasn't sure if he wanted to reveal climbing the mountain and meeting Sophia. "I don't know, just intuition, I guess. So, am I nice?"

"Sure," Jonathan answered. He took a deep breath. "Yes, you're nice. But of course there is more to you than that. You're also…" he struggled to find a word, and then said, "I don't spend much time thinking about this sort of thing. You're putting me on the spot."

"It's okay. You've helped me just fine," Thomas answered. It saddened Thomas to think that his closest friend could only describe him in superficial terms.

Jonathan stood and looked at Thomas for a minute before he added, "Brigitta wanted me to invite you and Lena and the kids over for dinner Friday night. Could you check if that would work and let me know?"

"That sounds great. I mean, that would be nice," Thomas chuckled, and Jonathan smiled.

When Thomas got home from work that evening, he went directly to Anna's room and kissed her on the forehead. "I love you, princess. Did you have a good day?"

She breathed in and then out, "Yes…" It was obvious that Anna's breathing was becoming more and more labored.

"Get some rest, honey. Dinner will be soon."

Anna smiled, though Thomas could see pain in her eyes. She looked exhausted. Shouldn't she be getting better? He closed her door behind him and then stopped at the boys' room where they were playing.

"Hey, Andrew, Erik, I've got a weird question I'd like to ask you."

"Sure, Dad," Andrew replied, while Erik kept playing with his toy horse.

"What do you boys think about me?"

Erik immediately answered without looking up, "You are the best dad ever. You are strong and powerful and you like to eat a lot."

His innocence and enthusiasm made Thomas grin. "Thanks, Erik. Good answer. Andrew?"

"What exactly do you mean?" Andrew asked thoughtfully.

"I'm wondering what you think when you think about me," Thomas said.

"You work a lot. And a lot of times when I'm trying to tell you something, you seem like you're thinking about something else. Like you're never really here in your head."

Thomas was stunned. *He is only eight*, he thought. Honesty was exactly what he had hoped to get, but he didn't think it would hurt. "That is a great answer, Andrew," Thomas swallowed, feeling like he was just hit in the face with a hefty bag of potatoes. "Anything else?"

"Nope, but I'll let you know," Andrew said, going back to playing with his brother.

"Okay. Good." He hesitated, not quite knowing what to say next. "I guess I'll see you at dinner then." He closed the door to their room and followed the enticing smells to find Lena in the kitchen.

"How did it go this morning? You left so early. Was she there?" Lena asked while mashing potatoes. "What did she say about Anna?"

"Lena, she was, and it was good. It was really good. But I think this is going to be more difficult than I first thought," Thomas said, sitting down at the table.

"What do you mean? The climbing?"

Thomas laughed. "No. This lady, Sophia—she seems to think there's some stuff about me that needs fixing before she can fix Anna."

"Do we have that much time?" Lena teased.

"Lena…"

"I'm sorry. I'm kidding. This is all very strange to me right now."

"I know, me too."

"What did she say? What's wrong with you?"

"That's an interesting question, Lena. Because she wanted me to ask you that."

"What?"

"She wanted me to ask people what they think about me. Lena, I know you love me. I know you think I'm crazy."

Lena smiled.

"But, what do you see deep down, deep inside of me—maybe something I can't even see myself?"

Lena kept preparing supper, but Thomas could see her trying to think of an answer to his question. After a moment of quiet, Thomas offered, "I just asked the boys what they thought about me." He told her what Andrew had said about seeming to be somewhere else in his head. "Is that true?" Thomas asked, trying not to appear as desperate as he felt.

She came and sat down next to Thomas. She reached out her hand, rested it on top of his, and looked him deep in the eyes. "I can certainly understand why he would say those things."

"Please tell me there's a 'but' coming."

"But I have to agree with him," she said.

"You do?"

"Yes, I do. Please understand, I'm not mad at you, and I don't think you're a bad father."

As much as he didn't want the whole truth, he knew it was what he needed to find for Sophia's assignment. *This is why we stay out of people's business. And apparently other people's business has been keeping track of my faults*, Thomas thought, and suddenly wished Benjamin were there. Benjamin would have loved all this.

Lena grasped his hand a bit tighter. "Each of us wishes things were different around here."

Thomas dropped his head and pulled his hand away from hers.

"These questions?" Lena asked. "I'm not sure they're good for you right now. It's hard for you to hear the answers."

"I can't ignore them any longer," Thomas' voice rose. "This isn't easy. As much as I don't want to ask these questions, I have to. For Anna." Thomas thought for the first time in his life, *maybe she's right…the whole village is right. The rules…we shouldn't talk about things like this.*

Lena's tone changed, as if she was trying to be more helpful now. "Since you asked, I have been wanting to talk to you about your lack of help around the house."

"Lena—can't you see I'm hurting here?"

"You're the one who asked," she said, with a rare display of defensiveness.

"Yes, but did you really think I wanted you to be honest?" Thomas said, trying to pass it off as irony. But instead of diffusing the tension, it only intensified it.

"If saving Anna means telling you the truth, then I will."

He pulled his chair closer to hers and looked deep into her eyes. "We are in this together. I need you. I need your help, even if it hurts," he said. "I don't know what Sophia is doing. But I have to complete her assignments. This is for our daughter."

"Since we're in this together, Thomas," Lena began, "I'm going to need you to be patient with me too. You go to meet a stranger on the mountain and then come back and ask odd questions. I can't help but feel a little unsettled."

Thomas was feeling a lot of emotions all at once: frustration, sadness, and impatience, like he wanted to cry or yell at the top of his lungs.

Lena continued. "I just hope it means you're coming to life. The life we have here in this house. This is where you're needed." She stood from the table and went back to working on the final preparations for their meal.

Thomas sat, thinking. *Why did I want to know what people think? If I'm not who I thought I was, then who am I? How is this supposed to help Anna?*

There was a delicious aroma from the beef Lena had been roasting all day. Fresh bread had just come out of the oven. And candles were burning on the table, hoping to set the mood for a cozy dinner. And even though Thomas felt like running, he knew the smartest choice would be to stay seated in the chair where he had just been grilled. He looked out the window; dusk was settling on the neighborhood. And as he saw the fingerlike branches of the trees moving in the breeze, buds just beginning to show themselves, Thomas longed to hear Sophia's singing. He longed to know that the path he was on was leading through all this pain to somewhere beautiful.

Tucking in Anna that evening, Thomas asked, "Princess, do you mind if I ask you a strange question?"

"Anything…Daddy," Anna replied, taking her time with each syllable.

"What kind of dad do you think I am?"

She struggled to catch her breath, and then said, "You're… the best."

Thomas leaned down and hugged his daughter.

"Anna, I know I'm not perfect. But I want to get better. I want to be a better dad to you and Andrew and Erik. So if you ever think of anything, you let me know, okay?"

She nodded. "Love you…Daddy."

"Love you too, princess."

TWELVE

Thomas awoke the next morning to the familiar sound of birds singing and knew Sophia would be waiting for him on the mountain. He kissed a still-sleeping Lena on the cheek as he hurried out of the house. Closing the front door behind him, he paused, remembered his kids, and went back inside, first to the boys' room.

He slowly opened the door and watched them sleep for a short while. He sensed the peace that filled the room and longed for some of his own. *All is right in their world*, he thought. *At least for this moment.* He kissed the boys on their foreheads, did the same to a peacefully sleeping Anna, and left the house.

Sophia was waiting for him, just as he expected. "I was just praying for you, Thomas."

"Oh, really? What were you praying?"

"For courage and bravery," Sophia replied.

"For me?"

"Yes, for you," she replied, then grinned.

Thomas wrinkled his brow and tried to imagine why Sophia would think he might need courage or bravery. "You must have a difficult assignment for me," he guessed.

"My prayer is not for a specific task or assignment you are going to face, but for a daily decision you must make—a daily decision to do what is right and true, no matter how afraid you may be."

Thomas nodded. "I can do that."

"You make me proud when you say things like that," Sophia said. "I will tell you a secret," she continued. "Feelings, especially fear, have a way of controlling a person's life more than they can even imagine. Feelings tell you to do what is most comfortable, not what is most right."

"Do I have a problem with this?" Thomas tried not to sound defensive.

"Son, everyone has a problem with this. It's the people who figure out how to experience the highs and lows of life through their feelings, without being controlled by them, who can most understand the mysteries of life."

"Do you think I'm letting my feelings control my decisions?" Thomas asked.

"First, I want to hear how it went with your assignment," Sophia said. "What do people think of you?"

Being with Sophia made Thomas think about his father. Perhaps it was because she was gentle yet seemed to be so fully in control—a graceful strength, just like his dad. He greatly admired his father who, when Thomas was only ten, died from a heart attack. His greatest memories came from time he spent watching him work in the shop or going for walks together on the outskirts of the village.

Thomas remembered his father's shoes, covered with dirt and years of wear, as well as his tree-trunk–like legs. The belt his father had worn revealed his amazing handiwork with tools. The buckle had a picture of a canoe resting in the middle of a lake surrounded by a dozen intricate trees, all hammered into the metal. Thomas would spend hours trying to imagine what the canoe and the lake would look like in real life, and he hoped one day to see the place his father etched from memory. Lake Holderen was a close approximation, but not exactly. His dad had said it was a lake far away from Bergland, which might have been his dad's attempt to help young Thomas think beyond the confines of their tiny village.

Also, the belt was just plain useful. His father had always said, "Even the strongest man needs help to hold his pants up." His father's upper body had widened out to his shoulders, with arms extending like two giant branches. Strong and muscular, his arms could have pulled a whole tree out by its roots—at least that is what Thomas told the other boys at school.

Thomas had been continually amazed at the whiskers that tickled whenever his father kissed him. When Thomas had walked past his father as he sat reading his newspaper or a book, he had run his hand along his father's cheek to feel the rough, stubbly beard. That had been a source of great comfort for young Thomas. It had allowed him to touch his father and express the closeness he felt for him. He had found it difficult to believe he would one day have a beard just like his dad.

His father's eyes were what Thomas remembered most. He could look up at his father and know exactly what he was feeling, be it anger, joy, or, most of the time, tremendous love. Thomas would never forget how his father would stand over him with a gleam in his eye that spoke volumes about the fondness he had for his son. Instead of using his height or strength to intimidate or frighten, his father would stand as tall as he could, chest puffed out, hands on his hips, and he would proudly say, "I not only love you, Thomas, but I really like you a lot." He would then crouch down to his son's level, completely envelope him in his arms, and hold him close. The boy never felt more protected.

Thomas had kept his father's belt after he died, and, even though he still had it in the drawer next to his bed, he had never worn it. He wasn't his father, after all. He just didn't feel worthy.

Sophia sat quietly while Thomas considered how to best answer her question. A tear formed in his eye.

"When you are facing a painful question, what do you think about, Thomas?" she asked with visible compassion.

"My father. I try to think about what my father might do," Thomas replied. "He always did the right thing. He was so strong and always knew how to handle everything."

"And that is how you would like to be?" she asked.

"I'm tired of being afraid that someone is going to find out I don't know what I am doing," Thomas confessed, with more anger than sorrow. "I feel like I'm somehow to blame for what happened to my daughter. And I'm supposed to be holding everything together, and I just can't do it. I've got it figured out just enough to be fooling everybody for now, but the day is coming when I'll be found out."

"Found out to be what?" Sophia said.

"I have no idea," he answered. Thomas looked into Sophia's eyes and saw that she had a stern look on her face.

"Are you afraid of somebody finding out that you need help getting through this little journey called life?" Her voice was surprisingly gentle.

Thomas looked up to the sky, and a tear fell down his cheek.

A bird flew over their heads, delivering its musical call, everything perfect in its world.

"Will you help me, Sophia?" Thomas asked.

"Yes, Thomas," she said. "We will help you." Sophia pointed to the top of the mountain and smiled.

Thomas released a huge sigh and closed his eyes. He still wasn't the man he wanted to be, but he wasn't alone anymore.

THIRTEEN

Thomas and Sophia settled underneath the overhang, which provided the best vantage point to see the sun rising over the village, bringing trees and houses to life with its light. He told Sophia everything he had learned about himself from the first assignment.

"What surprised you most about their responses?" Sophia asked.

"It surprised me that my best friend, Jonathan, could not say anything more about me than that I was nice. But it didn't surprise me, as much as I wish it would have, to hear what my oldest boy, Andrew, told me about how I never appear to listen to him." He paused. "I was most shocked by Lena, my wife."

"What did you expect her to say?"

"I have no idea," Thomas answered. Sophia let the silence linger. Finally, he said, "I just wish she would tell me the things I do that bother her right when they happen, instead of waiting and keeping everything inside."

"But you're keeping things inside too," Sophia said.

"But if she would just tell me what she wants, I would be glad to do it."

"Lena does not believe that, or else she already would have."

"Can we pretend this is all her problem?" Thomas asked hopefully.

"Thomas, God has made you in a specific manner. Along the way, however, through a series of choices you made, you became who you now are. If you want to change, it's not too late. You can decide who you want to become." She smiled. "It's your turn to take charge of who you are and what other people see. Hopefully it will be the same person in the end."

Thomas managed a tiny smile. "Sophia, sometimes you make my head spin," he confessed.

"Remember when I told you that 'whoever would dare to climb the mountain would be met with help from above'?"

"Yes," Thomas said.

"You are climbing a mountain that is larger than the piece of rock we are sitting on. You are traveling on a path most people never even attempt because it is so difficult. It is time to receive the help you asked for."

Thomas looked around where they were sitting, thinking Sophia was going to give him a gift or package of some sort. Instead, Sophia held out her hands in front of Thomas.

"Open your hands," she said, with a serious look, as if she were beginning a ceremony.

Thomas held out his open hands.

"I have told you a lot of things. But this one thing, I want you to tell to everyone you can, but only after you truly understand what it means for yourself."

His hands began to shake slightly. Thomas looked at them, hoping Sophia would not see. She reached out and took hold.

"I have told you the secret to the life you are looking for is found in letting go," Sophia said. Thomas nodded in agreement. "These open hands represent your admitted need for help. So many people try to fill them with all kinds of things, things that look important or valuable, just so they never have to see how empty their hands really are. Whenever you look down at your empty hands, remember: on your own you have nothing."

Sophia reached into her pocket and pulled out a ring, a solid band of gold, which reflected the rising sun as she held it high above Thomas' hands.

"This ring is to continually remind you that you are never, ever alone." She placed the gold band on his ring finger, opposite from his wedding band. "Whatever mountain you face, and wherever your path may lead, you can look at the ring and know that you are never alone."

"Sophia…" Thomas did not know what to say. Sophia held a finger to her mouth, silencing him.

"We have our secret place here, and God is with us," she continued. "But when you go down from the mountain, God is still with you, longing for you to be in a relationship with him—a relationship that will allow you to find the life you are looking for."

"How do you have a relationship with God? Go to church every day?"

Sophia laughed. "No, son. You do not have to go to church to meet with God. He is with you wherever you go. As with any relationship, it is important to communicate. God wants to know your thoughts and your feelings, and he wants you to know his. As you begin to understand more about what God says about you, your entire life will be different. His wise heart will change yours; his character will change your character."

Thomas felt his brows knitting, and Sophia shook her head gently.

"It's okay if you don't understand all this right now," she reassured him. "It is a process of understanding that will continue for the rest of your life, if you let it. When you feel helpless, or like life isn't going the way you think it should, I want you to look at your ring. Let go of everything you think you need to hold on to so tightly. Ask for the help you need and trust that God is with you."

Thomas thought about his father and wondered what he would think about this fantastical mountainside scene. He pictured himself as a young boy, with his father holding him close, remembering how he felt surrounded and protected by his father's arms. Feeling his father's strength made him feel strong even then. Now as a grown man, admitting his weaknesses—one of the most frightening things he could do—was leading him to a source of strength and comfort he never imagined.

"My father…" Thomas choked up.

Sophia added, "…is very proud of you."

Lowering his eyes to the ground, he stopped at the sight of the new ring on his hand. It sparkled as Thomas wondered what it might feel like to actually let go of everything he was holding on to. But if he did, who would save Anna?

FOURTEEN

Thomas couldn't wait to tell his wife about his new gift. He pictured her smiling face and warm embrace after telling her about this new love he found, or rather, received.

"I better get home. I'd love to give Anna a big kiss. And help my wife get the boys ready for school." Thomas looked at the ring, and then at Sophia. "I have never said those words in my whole life," he added with a tone of surprise.

Sophia smiled.

"Before I leave, do you have another assignment for me?" Thomas said hesitantly.

She thought for a moment. "Yes. I want you to think about what kind of relationship you want to have with God."

"You mean, I get to decide?"

"Everybody gets to decide what kind of relationship they are going to have with God. That's the beautiful part of it all," Sophia grinned. "God seldom imposes himself on anyone. He stands at the door of your life and knocks. You can open the door and talk to him on occasion, invite him in to stay, or simply never answer."

"I am the one in control?" he asked.

She hesitated. "It is like a person standing on the shore of the ocean. The waves are huge and the water is deep. You can't control the ocean. Still, the water calls you to jump in and swim as much as you desire. It never forces you to jump in. The ocean simply offers its water."

"I'm not much of a swimmer," Thomas said with a smile. "But you want me to decide how far out I want to swim?"

"You can get just your feet wet, or you can dive in and get completely lost in the flow of the water," Sophia replied.

"In everyday language, what does that mean?"

"You can spend as much time as you desire with the other person. You can decide how much you tell the other person about your life. You decide what influence you allow the other person to have. It is the same with God."

"But I can't see him," Thomas said.

"Yes, but you can see your ring, correct?"

"Of course."

"Just like that ring, God is real and always with you," Sophia said. "But there is a difference between the symbol and the Divine. You can take the ring off, but neither you, nor anything else, will ever be able to separate you from the love of God."

"Do you mean there is nothing I could do to make God stop loving me?"

"Nothing, no matter what you do, even if you sometimes feel like he has," she told him. "But that gets us back to the whole issue of not letting your feelings decide the truth."

"Thank you, Sophia," Thomas said. "Your gift is more beautiful and more meaningful than I could've ever dreamed."

"The real gift I have given you is not something to place on your hand. It is something that has been placed in your heart. An enemy could cut off your head, or burn down your house, or even take away your family—everything that means so much. But no one can ever take away what is in your heart."

Thomas moved toward Sophia and hugged her tightly, the first time he had ever embraced her. "But what about my daughter?"

"I must go," she said, gently pulling away.

"But you promised…"

"And you must return to the village. Your life is there with your family and your friends. Anna is waiting for you. I will see you again, son."

"Sophia…"

She again placed her finger to her lips to silence him, turned around, and began the walk down her usual path around the mountain. Thomas stood still, certain that Sophia must be an angel.

The next time they met, he would ask her just that.

FIFTEEN

Walking back down the mountain, Thomas was over-whelmed with emotions. He was frustrated that Sophia never said anything about Anna getting better. But, in spite of that, he couldn't wait to see Lena and the kids. He began brain-storming ways they could join him on this journey. How could he make the idea of a relationship with God real for them? Is that what he was supposed to bring to Anna, a kind of spiritual healing? That didn't seem like enough for a father to offer his sick child.

He paused in the middle of the path, looked up to the sky, and prayed, "God, I am not exactly sure what you are doing, but I like it. I feel like I can enjoy life for the first time, and you know that it's far from perfect. I can love the people around me more, though. I can enjoy being by myself more. Please feel free to keep doing whatever you are doing. But don't forget that Anna needs you. We all need you now."

Thomas wondered if being so casual with God was

disrespectful, but then he smiled as he remembered how Sophia told him God just wants to know what we feel.

"And God," he continued, "please don't let me ever get so religious that I know all the right words to say. Amen."

Arriving at his house, Thomas stopped just in front of the kitchen window and caught a glimpse of his kids and wife inside. He stood to the side so they couldn't see him. He watched as they ate their breakfast and talked to their mother. The boys laughed. Anna appeared to smile as she sat reclined in her wheelchair. *They look so happy*, Thomas thought. Lena affectionately ran her hand through Andrew's hair, and he smiled up at her.

Thomas entered through the front of the house, just in time to catch the boys running past the front door toward their room.

"Daddy," the boys screamed, as they turned and lunged forward to hug Thomas.

"I sure do love you boys," he said.

"Me too, Dad," Andrew answered softly.

"Me three, Dad!" Erik shouted.

"Are you ready for school?" Thomas asked them.

"Yes, sir," they answered, and ran off to their room for their books and jackets.

Lena approached Thomas in the front hallway, wheeling Anna to sit near the fireplace with its picture window on the left. "They sure are excited to see you."

"I know," he said, not wanting to appear too surprised. He leaned down and kissed Anna on the forehead. "I love you so much, my princess!"

"I love…you, too…Daddy."

Thomas smiled at his daughter but looked up at Lena with sadness in his eyes.

Lena smoothed Anna's hair and then stared at Thomas, a puzzled expression on her face.

"What are you doing?" he chuckled.

"There is something different in your eyes," she said. She paused, and then asked, "What's going on inside of you, Thomas?"

"Only good," he answered as the boys ran back to the front door. "Have a great day at school today, okay?" Thomas told them.

"Yes, sir," they replied.

"And if you get in trouble, try to make it look like it was the other person's fault."

"Thomas," Lena exclaimed, slapping him on the shoulder.

"Yes, sir," they giggled in unison, hugging their parents and scampering out the front door.

Lena moved Anna to sit near the window and returned to Thomas, offering, "How about a cup of coffee?"

"I'd love that," he replied as they walked toward the kitchen.

As they sat, Lena remained quiet, perhaps to see if he would begin the conversation.

"Lena, do you believe in God?" Thomas asked, thinking it would be a safe place to start.

"Doesn't everybody?" she answered, pouring the coffee from the pot on the table.

"But you, Lena, do *you* believe in God?"

She sighed. "What's your point?"

"What I am trying to ask is, what kind of relationship do you have with God?"

"I wonder if that is actually possible," she admitted. "It seems to me that having a relationship with someone implies they care about you, and I can't help but wonder if God cares about us. I know I'm supposed to believe he does. But what about Anna? If God cared, wouldn't she be healthy?"

Thomas nodded. That was a hard question. "Lena, you

asked what is going on with me. This is what is going on: I am starting to believe God wants us to feel his love—no matter what happens to us. So when bad things, or good things, happen, he is there to help us and to love us. I think that's what hope is. Not a hope that circumstances will change, but a hope that we won't be left alone in them."

"I'm not so sure about that," Lena said. "I feel alone, every day."

"But why?" he asked.

She wiped at her eyes with the back of her hand, as if she didn't want him to see her tears.

Thomas looked down at his new ring and took a deep breath and a new approach, one of humility. "Lena, I love you very much. I'm so sorry for everything I have done that has kept me at a distance from you. I've been busy, by my own choosing, and my relationship with you and the kids has suffered. And I believe it's hindered you from being able to see how much God truly loves you as well." He swallowed and looked Lena intently in the eyes. "You are a wonderful wife. I could not ask for anything more from you. Please forgive me for not seeing your pain and not being here when you needed me."

Lena's eyes widened. She slowly shook her head, as if in disbelief.

Thomas stood up, grabbed Lena's hand, and pulled her into an embrace, startling her. She stood limp-armed at first, but when she realized Thomas wasn't letting go, she slowly wrapped her arms around him. After a moment, he took her face into his hands and drew it so close to his own face that he felt her breath and smelled her perfume. With his warm hands he held her delicately, like she was made of china. He looked at every part of her face. Her eyes were the same blue that he fell in love with when they first met, even though they were beginning to show signs of age around the corners. Thomas ran his thumbs across her upper lip first, starting in the center and moving outward; then the bottom lip. He felt a slight quiver as he touched them.

He could have kissed her at this point, but instead he spoke softly. "I am finished loving you the way I have been. If you'll let me, I have a new love to give you." Thomas knew the words he was speaking were not his own. He continued, "It is a love that goes beyond what I can even understand. It is a love that says I will never leave you. I am no longer the most important thing in my life. It also means I'm willing to give more of me to you than I ever imagined possible. This is the love I want to give you."

They kissed, and it felt like their first kiss, and maybe it was.

"Of course, only if you are interested," he added with a gentle smirk.

"I'm very interested."

They laughed, and Thomas caught Anna watching them. He gave her a little wink, and she laughed too.

Sixteen

As he walked to his shop, Thomas couldn't help but grin. Although still weighed down with grief over Anna's illness, he was beginning to trust that God was going to take care of her. He was also thrilled about his time together with Lena. He wasn't exactly sure what made their time together such a success. Their conversation about God wasn't particularly amazing. Something happened, though, when he apologized to her. It was as if saying "I am sorry" was what he needed to free himself to tell Lena he loved her. Maybe she needed to hear his regret before she could hear his love.

He decided from that day forward to make a coffee date part of their day-to-day routine. During his free time in the shop, Thomas made a couple of personalized mugs for himself and Lena.

While he worked, Thomas caught sight of the ring on his hand. He stopped what he was doing and took a moment to try talking with God.

"God," he began, "I don't know quite what to say to you, and sorry it's taken me so long. But 'thanks' seems to be a good place to start." He looked around for things to say thanks for. "Thanks for giving me this shop. Sure, it was handed down through the years, and many times I thought it was actually a curse rather than a blessing…But it has been really good for me to have this place to come each day and use my hands to make things for other people." Thomas felt a little silly talking to an empty shop, but hopefully in time this would be easier.

"Thanks for Lena and her incredible heart. Thanks for giving her patience to be able to put up with me. And about these assignments with Sophia…I look forward to you doing your part in helping Anna get better. Thank you in advance. Thanks for blessing us with Anna and for Andrew and Erik." Thomas paused a moment. "Please protect them today. And help me to be the father they need. I want to show them how much I love them—something I know I am going to need your help to do."

Thomas closed his eyes and for the first time pictured his oldest, Andrew, as a man, talking to his own son about his father. He heard him speak about how his father never listened to him and always seemed like he was somewhere else.

My father tried really hard to be good man, but he was not able to figure out how to be the father I needed, Thomas imagined his son saying. *I just wanted to know he would be there for me not only when I needed him, but also even when I just wanted to be with him.*

He would not let this daydream turn into a reality.

The door to his shop opened and in walked Isaac. "Good morning," Thomas said.

"Hello, Thomas."

"I have your wife's new pot all ready. I wrapped it nicely for you to give it to her."

Isaac frowned, seeming a bit stunned. "Thank you so much, Thomas. I…"

Thomas waved his hand to silence Isaac. "It was my pleasure."

"Do you mind if I sit down for a minute?" Isaac asked as he pulled up a chair to Thomas' workbench.

"Of course not. What's going on?"

"Oh, not a whole lot," he answered, but Thomas noticed that he didn't look him in the eye as he said it.

Thomas sat silent, waiting.

"That's not completely true," Isaac confessed. "Remember how you asked me the question wondering about how you come across to people?"

"Of course I do."

"Well, I haven't been able to stop thinking about that."

"Do you have a better answer for me today?"

"To be honest, I haven't been thinking about you at all. I've been thinking about me."

Thomas smiled as Isaac continued. "It has been driving me a bit crazy because I don't think people could even say that I am nice. I don't think people know me at all, except maybe that I'm a farmer out in the field all day. That doesn't seem right, for people not to know me. I grew up here, after all."

Thomas thought this might be a good time to take another chance with Isaac. "Let me ask you this, Isaac. Have you ever talked to God about this?"

Isaac furrowed his eyebrows.

"It's just a thought," Thomas added.

"You know I go to church," Isaac said. "I see you there every Sunday. But God can't be at all interested in me personally. Why would God care about how I come across to other people?"

"Well, recently, I've come to believe he does," Thomas answered him with confidence that surprised even himself. "I also know God wants to hear what is going on inside of you, like your thoughts and feelings, and he wants you to know his too. It is very similar to the relationship you have with your wife."

"I'm not sure I believe all that," Isaac said. "Not yet, anyway. But do you think he'd help me change the way other people see me?"

"I can't answer that for you—only God knows what he is going to do in your life. But if you let him, he'll change you. I'm certain."

"Interesting thoughts, Thomas," Isaac said as he stood. "Thanks." He and Thomas shook hands, and Isaac grabbed the wrapped pot before he walked toward the door.

"I didn't really answer your question," Thomas said suddenly. "But perhaps there's another question that might need to be answered first."

"What's that?" Isaac asked, turning back toward Thomas.

"Exactly what kind of relationship would you want to have with God?"

Isaac scratched his chin for a moment before answering. "That is a very good question, Thomas. But for now, I really have to get home. Oh, and thanks for the new pot." He turned back to the door and hurried out, avoiding eye contact.

The door closed, leaving Thomas alone once again.

"You are welcome," he said to himself.

"God, I'm not sure what just happened here," Thomas prayed. "But I do ask that you will show yourself to Isaac and let him know how much you love him. And help him, and me, to understand that other people's opinions aren't what really matters. What matters is whether the people we love really know us at all."

In a flash, Sophia's first and second assignments suddenly made sense. Thomas could only discover the person he was meant to be by deciding what kind of relationship he wanted to have with God. If he was transparent with God, then he could be open with the people he loved too. And maybe Anna's mission in sending him up the mountain was not so much about her healing, but his.

Thomas could now become the man he was always supposed to be. But would God allow Thomas to find life, even if Anna lost hers?

SEVENTEEN

Throughout the remainder of the day in the shop, Thomas' thoughts turned back to his kids. His determination to make a positive impact on them as a father, and eventually as a friend, continued to grow. Getting used to the idea of telling God what he was thinking, Thomas prayed out loud.

"You know how much I love my kids," Thomas said. "And while I haven't been the greatest at showing them how I feel, now is a good time for me to make some changes in how I treat them. But I need your help—because I have no idea what I'm supposed to do."

Even though his eyes were open the entire time he was talking, when he finished, he looked around the room to see if anything was different. It was completely silent. Nothing had changed. The wood beams overhead, the workbench, the tools, all exactly where they had been. He didn't feel anything inside of him change. He certainly didn't feel like God had revealed anything to him about how to better handle his kids, and he wondered if he ever would. Thomas sat in the silence for a short while, hoping for a signal of some kind that would prove God was listening. Nothing.

"I am going to trust that you are in control," Thomas said finally. "And that even when you don't give me a response when I want it, you're going to lead me toward your answer."

That's when something changed. Thomas immediately felt a release of the tension that had been building up inside. He did not have any answers, but he felt calm and peaceful, and somehow he knew that everything was going to work out. He did not even know what to call this new feeling, only that he had a new inner certainty, even in the midst of the external unknown.

At dinner that evening, Lena and Thomas sat in their usual places across the table from the boys and Anna. Lena had made a giant batch of the kids' favorite seafood stew. And there were St. Lucia buns—eggy sweet rolls scented with saffron—a rare treat for later.

They were all entertained by the boys' recounting the activities of the day. Even if it was merely about the games they made up on the playground during school, Thomas saw so much life in their eyes.

"And then..." Erik described in detail what his friend did to a girl on the playground. "...Soren went up to her..." He took a bite of his food and continued, "And he rumpled it wif a hap an roobied it to da harg!" Erik swallowed the food that was in his mouth. "Can you believe it? It's true! I was there!"

Thomas and Lena shared a smile as Anna giggled.

"Erik, that is unbelievable!" Thomas said.

"I know," Erik's head bobbed.

"Andrew, how about you?" Thomas asked. "How was your day?"

"Fine," the boy answered, keeping his head lowered and his eyes on his food.

Thomas looked to Lena, raising his eyebrows as if to ask her, *did something happen?* She shook her head and shrugged.

"What did you do today?" Thomas asked.

Andrew looked up at his father with a face filled with sadness and confusion. "Dad, why do you climb the mountain?"

Anna's eyes widened.

Thomas sat down his fork and knife. "What are you talking about?" He had no idea anyone else besides Lena knew about his trips up the mountain.

"They were talking about you on the playground today, about how you climb the mountain. They all said you're crazy."

Thomas tried to imagine who had been watching him each day.

"They said anyone who climbs the mountain never comes back because they die. I don't want you to die." Andrew began to cry.

Thomas got up from his seat, moved to the other side of the table, and held his son in his arms. "I am not going to die, Andrew. Don't worry."

"Is it true? Is it?" Andrew asked through his sobs.

Thomas pulled his chair around the table to sit down next to his son. "Yes. I do climb the mountain. But it's a good thing," Thomas continued.

"Really? How is it a good thing?" Andrew looked up at him angrily.

Thomas looked over at Lena, at Anna and Erik, then back at Andrew. "All the people who say that climbing the mountain is crazy, they don't know what they're talking about. This village has some strange ways of looking at things. Ignorant people are always looking to justify their fears and insecurities. And this glorious, awesome mountain is nothing to be afraid of."

"But haven't people died climbing it?" Andrew asked.

"Those are just rumors. Anything to keep people from dreaming, from thinking about how much better life could be than simply settling for keeping things the way they have always been. I'm tired of living that way."

"Brave..." Anna whispered.

"Thank you, princess." Thomas smiled at his daughter.

"But Dad, how can you be brave doing something so scary?" Andrew wondered.

He looked at his daughter, "Anna?"

"Love..." Anna exhaled.

Lena's eyes widened.

Thomas nodded slowly. "Yes, that's right. I can be brave because of love. Just like you can be. Whenever you're scared, just remember how loved you are by me, your mother...and God too. God loves you so much. He makes us all brave."

Lena finally spoke. "Your father is at a place in life where he's trying to figure out how to be the best dad, the best husband, and the best man he can be. Climbing the mountain is a great help for him. And we all know he needs a lot of help." Lena winked at Thomas, and they all laughed.

Andrew still looked puzzled. "How is climbing a mountain helping you with that?"

Thomas took a deep breath and sat up straighter in his chair. "I have made a friend on the mountain, someone who knows a lot more about this life than I could ever know."

"Is this friend a man or a woman?" Andrew asked, a dark cloud in his eyes. Thomas imagined he was thinking about his friend whose father had abandoned the family for another woman.

"Her name is Sophia."

"Oh," Andrew dropped his head.

"And she is probably eighty years old," he quickly added.

"Does she live up there?" Andrew asked. His face brightened considerably.

"Honestly, I'm not sure where she lives."

"Do we get to meet her?" Erik asked enthusiastically.

"Yes, when do we get to meet this friend of yours?" Lena said.

"I'm not sure. But it would be great if you could," Thomas answered. "I was going to ask Andrew, since he's the oldest, if he would be interested in going up the mountain with me tomorrow morning."

"You promise that we're not going to die?" Andrew asked.

"Of course, I promise. We have to leave pretty early to make it up the mountain and back before you miss too much of school."

"The mountain isn't dangerous or scary?" Andrew asked.

"Turns out it's not. Sometimes we grow up believing things that aren't completely true."

"Great." Andrew rose and began to dart from the table. "I'll be up early."

"Andrew," Thomas said sternly, causing the boy to stop in his tracks and turn toward his father.

"I'm sorry. May I be excused?"

"Yes, you may. You too, Erik." Andrew dashed off, his little brother following closely behind.

"Honey, he is only eight. Are you sure it is safe?" Lena said when they were gone.

"He'll be fine. I'll be right there to help along the entire way. And between you and me," he continued, moving in closer to Lena, "I found a way up the mountain that is not too difficult."

"Maybe it is not for a grown man, but for an eight-year-old, Thomas?"

"Trust me."

"With the life of my son?"

"He's my son, too, Lena. And yes, you can trust me. I will never let him leave my sight," Thomas said. He wished Lena could believe that he wanted only the very best for Andrew.

Thomas stared at her, as if he could will her to understand his heart and finally trust him completely.

Lena sighed and stood, following the boys out of the room, leaving Thomas in the kitchen with Anna.

He prayed silently, *God, Lena needs to trust me, and I need to trust you. Please help me, and please help her know everything is going to be all right.*

Thomas did not get the same peaceful feeling he had after his prayer earlier that day. Instead, he felt sick to his stomach.

Anna struggled to catch her breath and speak. "Daddy... what's...wrong?"

"Oh, honey. It's all going to be okay."

"Why...are you...sad?"

Thomas raised his head toward his daughter and noticed the dark circles under her little eyes. She looked exhausted. He reached his hand out to hold hers. "Sometimes it's really hard to be brave."

"You...climbed..."

"Yes, I did. And I will continue to, until you are well."

"Brave..." Anna said.

"Only because of love, Anna. Only because of love," Thomas replied.

"Love you…Daddy."

Thomas kissed her on the forehead, feeling its warmth, and then asked, "How do you do it, Anna? You are so brave, dealing with this terrible disease, always staying so happy and patient."

"I know…I'm going…to get better."

He squeezed her hand tighter. "Yes, you are, princess. Yes, you are."

Eighteen

Thomas leaned over his sleeping son to wake him. Andrew sprung from under the covers, fully clothed.

"Come on, Dad! Hurry up!" Andrew exclaimed and ran out of his room, leaving Thomas standing there startled.

Moments later, Lena met Thomas and Andrew by the front door, still appearing a bit nervous about their hike. She handed Thomas a backpack filled with food she had prepared. Thomas, still feeling a bit sick in his stomach, figured it best to not say anything to Lena about it. Only Andrew seemed thrilled at the adventure ahead.

"You don't have to tell us to be careful, Mother," Andrew said. "I will take care of Dad. He will be just fine." Thomas and Lena smiled at each other.

"And I promise," Thomas added, "if something horrible happens to Andrew, that I will drag him all the way down the mountain by his toenails." Andrew's eyes widened. "So we don't clutter up the mountain with his body."

"Not funny, Thomas," Lena warned.

"No, that wasn't very funny at all," Andrew added with a look of disgust.

"I was teasing, I promise. That's why I'm taking you up the mountain," Thomas said, leaning down to Andrew. "Because I believe you're big enough to handle anything that might happen. And in a few years, I'll take your brother."

"Please don't make Andrew miss too much school," Lena said. "I told his teacher you had a special field trip planned for this morning."

"Fantastic," Thomas replied, winking at his son. "We will go up the mountain, talk to Sophia for a couple of minutes, and be back before you can say 'poison ivy.'"

"Dad. I'm ready to go." Andrew sounded impatient. Lena leaned down to kiss her son on the forehead and hugged him tightly.

"Lena," Thomas began, "we will be fine. I promise."

She kissed Thomas and then watched them walk out the front door and down the front sidewalk to the street.

The first part of their climb was uneventful. "This is pretty easy, Dad," Andrew said, although they had not yet reached the point where the path began its steep ascent.

"It sure is a lot easier having you here with me," Thomas told his son. "But I have to tell you, Andrew, while it may be easy now, it's going to get a lot more difficult pretty soon."

"Oh, Dad. You'll be fine." Andrew responded.

"Thanks. I really needed to hear that." Thomas chuckled under his breath. He loved his son's confidence.

"And don't worry about me. I have really strong legs."

"That's a good thing, Andrew." Thomas said. "You got them from my side of the family."

As the climb became more precarious, Thomas wondered if it would be better to put his son in front of him to catch Andrew if he fell, or lead the way himself, testing the rocks and pathway for his son trailing in the rear. He decided to follow Andrew so he could keep an eye on his every move. Thomas followed closely to be able to catch his son if he were to stumble.

Climbing over large rocks and avoiding fallen tree limbs on the increasingly steep trail, young Andrew started to breathe heavily. "Dad...why..." Andrew tried to speak while he climbed. "Tell me again.... Why...do you...climb...the...mountain?"

Thomas stopped their climb for a minute and allowed his son to catch his breath. "It began by Anna asking me to try to climb it. I wanted to find a cure for her. Then I realized that maybe we all need some kind of cure," Thomas tried to explain. "It seems to me that everybody in Bergland wants to keep doing things the way they always have. But I don't. I have this thing... this hunger...inside my heart that tells me there's got to be something more to life. "

"I'm starting to feel a little hunger myself," Andrew said as he rubbed his stomach. They found a rock to sit on and opened up the backpack to see what food Lena had packed for them.

"What I have found is that the change that I'm looking for is actually inside of me, rather than in any of the people around me." Thomas was trying his best to explain his situation in a way his eight-year-old son could understand. Andrew was content to eat his sandwich, yet he appeared to catch at least a little of what his father said. "And what is happening," Thomas continued, "is that I'm learning more about what it means to be a good dad to you, Erik, and Anna, and a good husband to

Mother. I'm hoping that I'll find a way to cure Anna, but as I try, at least I can give her the father she deserved all along."

Thomas looked at his son and so desperately wanted to tell him about the nightmare he had and how he was determined to not let it come to reality. He also wanted to tell him about all the things he was learning in his heart—about how he was beginning to understand that God wanted to have a relationship with him. And how the climbing had something to do with getting Anna well but in ways he didn't understand yet. He also thought about his own father and the walks they used to take together.

Thomas couldn't remember anything specific his father had said to him during their times together. Instead, he clearly remembered the feeling of being best buddies with him—the feeling that his father thought the world of him and would do anything in his power to make his son happy. Thomas ruffled Andrew's hair. Thomas wanted to give that same gift to his own kids.

Was it possible that Anna wanted him to find this kind of peace, the peace of a life with no regrets, no matter what happened to her?

"Andrew, I want you to know how much I love you," Thomas said to his son, looking him in the eyes. "There is nothing you could do that would ever change that. Nothing you can do will make me love you less, and nothing you ever do will make me love you more."

"I have to go to the bathroom," Andrew said. He slid off the rock they were sitting on. "Come on, Dad. Let's go."

Sighing, Thomas gathered up the remaining food, returned it to the backpack, and slipped off the rock and onto the trail. Maybe this time was more for him than Andrew. Besides, Andrew knew how to live in the moment.

Andrew didn't seem to worry about anything in the past

or be too concerned about the future. He just lived in the present. *When did I lose that?* Thomas thought to himself. Maybe Thomas needed to follow Andrew's lead in more ways than he knew.

God, are you trying to tell me something here? Thomas prayed silently while they walked. *Is this all about me and how I should stop worrying about all I need to be in the future and be more grateful for what I have already become? Or is this about Anna? Am I supposed to let go of worrying about what might happen to her in the future and simply be more present with her now?*

Thomas searched the sky for the birds that usually flew overhead. They always seemed to be a sign affirming his spiritual growth. This morning, all he heard was the crackling of twigs and leaves underneath his feet while he and Andrew walked. He looked up and saw the shadow of overhead branches against the increasingly blue sky. The branches were small, but each covered the endless sky beyond.

Thomas held his hand directly in front of him. He looked at the ring from Sophia and then spread his fingers apart, looked through them, and could see Andrew walking ahead of him. He opened and closed his fingers a couple of times, changing the perspective each time he opened them. Thomas could keep his eyes focused on his son, making his hand out of focus, even though it was closer.

God, Thomas began, *is my focus off? Please help keep my eyes focused on what you want me to see and not just on what I want to look at.*

Thomas felt a stirring in his belly. It wasn't hunger, but anxiety. He didn't know why. The thought crossed his mind that they could turn around and head back home. Andrew paused and looked back at Thomas, his face beaming with anticipation. Thomas took a deep breath.

He knew Sophia would be waiting, so they pressed on.

NINETEEN

They were nearly halfway to the secret place when Andrew whooped in delight. "Dad, look at this!"

He tore off into the rough weeds on the right side of the path. Thomas felt his heart skip a beat when he saw his son run off the trail. Andrew had seen something that caught his eye and ran so fast that Thomas had to work to keep up with him.

Andrew continued running for what felt to Thomas like two or three minutes. *Surely his vision is not that good*, Thomas thought. As Thomas' breathing became heavier and each step more and more challenging, it appeared as if Andrew was actually moving in slow motion—running and jumping over small obstacles, his hair flopping up and down. All Thomas could hear was the wind in his ears.

Thomas reached out to try and grab Andrew. He was just an arm's length out of reach when the boy jumped up, onto, and over a giant fallen tree. Thomas gasped at the sight and felt his stomach rise up into his throat. He could see nothing but blue sky beyond the row of trees that stood in line next to the fallen one. Thomas froze in his tracks, still surrounded by silence.

Then, desperate to see what had happened, Thomas pulled himself up onto the tree's rotting trunk. He was out of breath from running after his son, and what he saw took away any breath that remained.

It was the most glorious sight Thomas had ever seen.

Andrew had landed in the most enormous field of wild daisies—huge white petals with brilliant yellow centers. Thomas caught sight of Andrew about fifty yards away, leaping through the rows of flowers with wild abandon.

"How did you find this place?" he shouted.

"Come on, Dad, isn't it great?" Andrew called out.

"Wait for me," Thomas said, jumping off the tree and into the field, running after his son.

When he finally caught up with Andrew, Thomas grabbed his son's hands and began swinging him around in a circle.

"Faster, faster!" Andrew cried.

Thomas actually started spinning him so fast that Andrew's legs rose up off the ground and started to swing out away from him. His feet flew out over the tops of the flowers, occasionally skimming one or two with his toes. Andrew closed his eyes and held his mouth wide open as he was swung around.

"I'm flying! Dad, I'm flying," Andrew giggled.

"Yes, you are," Thomas said.

Andrew opened his eyes and looked straight at Thomas with a look of joy and wonder. Thomas slowed down their spinning and finally brought his son to rest on his feet. He let go of Andrew's hands, and they both fell backward into the flowers.

"It's so beautiful, isn't it?" Andrew said, lying on his back.

"I've never seen anything like this before," Thomas answered, inhaling the aroma of the flowers. "How did you know this was here, Andrew?"

"When we came around that last corner, I could see through the trees this big whiteness. I knew it had to be something beautiful."

"You scared the living daylights out of me when you ran off like that."

"I'm sorry, Dad," Andrew said.

"It's okay, buddy."

Thomas slowly realized he had no idea where they were or how to get back on the main path.

Like all the other inhabitants of Bergland, Thomas had always avoided difficult situations. The path of least resistance had never led him into danger, but there had never been any daisy fields along the way either.

Thomas knew they could try to find the main path or head straight in the direction of the top of the mountain, hoping to cross the original path in the process. Rather than backtracking, Thomas decided the best use of their time would be to head toward the mountaintop. He hoped Sophia would choose to wait.

Andrew and Thomas walked through the field of flowers until they reached the border of trees and brush, and then they turned around for one last look. From this view, the field looked even larger than before. They had obviously stumbled onto a plateau of some kind on the side of the mountain. With the flowers appearing to drop off the far edge of the mountain, it was impossible to see how far down the mountainside they continued.

"God is truly amazing," Thomas said to his son. "I've never found this place the whole time I've been on the mountain. But you found it the very first time you came here."

"It's a gift, Dad," Andrew said.

"It certainly is," Thomas replied.

Andrew reached down and picked one of the beautiful flowers. "Can we bring some home to Mom?"

"Sure, we can."

The boy grabbed a handful more, brushed off the dirt from the stems, and put them in the backpack. "Let's go find Sophia," Andrew said. Thomas was amazed the boy actually remembered her name.

"Wait. One thing before we get back to the path."

"What's that, Dad?"

"Turn to the open field and yell your name."

"My name?" Andrew asked.

"Yes. As loud as you can."

He cupped his hands around his mouth and yelled, "Annndrew!" The sound echoed off the trees and across the valley. His eyes widened—he'd never heard his own voice return back to him like this. Again he yelled, "Annndrew!" They laughed together at the joy of the moment. And then one last time the boy exclaimed, "I'm Annndrewwww! I climbed the mountain!"

Andrew looked up at his dad. "I bet the guys down in the village all heard that."

"I hope they did." Thomas put his arm around his son. *God, thanks for sending gifts in all shapes and sizes*, Thomas thought to himself, taking one last glance at the field of flowers, and then turning toward the trees, continued their journey up the mountain.

TWENTY

Thomas and Andrew continued along a new path for another fifteen minutes before the scenery began to appear familiar. "I recognize these trees, Andrew," Thomas said with excitement.

"They look like all the other trees," Andrew said.

"Yes, but something changes as we get higher and closer to Sophia. I think the trees are smaller."

They walked for a couple more minutes, until Thomas started running. "Come on!"

"What is it?" Andrew began running to keep up with his father.

"We're here." Thomas and Andrew were standing right in the middle of the secret clearing.

"This can't be the right place, Dad."

"Why is that?"

"There is no Sophia."

Thomas looked around, thinking Sophia might have left a message for him. He didn't find anything.

"Hey, Andrew, why don't we sit down for a minute?"

"Okay, Dad," he replied.

Thomas took the backpack off and sat it on the ground next to him. They sat with their backs against the side of the mountain and looked out over their village below. This was the place where Sophia gave him the ring.

"It sure is pretty," Andrew said.

Thomas nodded in agreement.

"Son, you know how we go to church every Sunday?"

"It's pretty boring, isn't it?"

"Yes it is, now that you mention it." They laughed together, and then Thomas became serious. "The church does a lot of good to help a person, that's for sure. But one thing that's always bothered me about church is that I never feel like I'm good enough. Or that I'm never able to do all the right things I'm supposed to do in order to be a good Christian. It's like playing a game that you know you can't win."

"Then why play?" Andrew said.

"Exactly. I don't want to play that game any longer. I want to learn how to have an actual relationship with God, one that has nothing to do with me being good enough."

"I think I'm getting hungry again."

Thomas chuckled, glad that Andrew never let things get too deep or serious or ever lost sight of the most important things in life, like food. He opened up the backpack and pulled out some of the food that remained after their first snack. "Before we eat, Andrew, how about we pray?"

"Pray?" Andrew furrowed his eyebrows.

"Yes. To God."

"Okay."

"Just tell God what you are thinking. It's pretty easy."

Andrew didn't close his eyes or fold his hands in typical

praying style. "God," Andrew began, looking up to the sky. "This is really fun. I like my dad." He looked at Thomas and they smiled at each other. "And I'm really happy to not be at school right now."

He waited a moment, and then said to Thomas, "That's all."

"Good job, son."

"Thanks, Dad. Now you go."

Thomas prayed in the same manner as his boy, "God, thank you for my wonderful son, Andrew, and Erik too, our beautiful Anna, and their mother. You have given us so much. I cannot say thank you enough. Please make Anna well, and soon. Thank you for keeping us safe this morning on our climb. Thank you for loving us." Thomas looked at Andrew and said, "That's all."

They both laughed.

Looking out over the village, Andrew said, "Things look so small from up here."

"It really is amazing," Thomas agreed, "how things seem so big when you are in the middle of them. But when you get a different view, things look much smaller."

"Is that how it is for you?"

"What do you mean?"

"When you leave us to go to work, do we get smaller when you get farther away?"

"Come here." Thomas reached out to embrace his son. "You will never get smaller to me, no matter where I go or whatever I do." Thomas heard a nearby bird whistling its morning greeting. "I keep you real big in my heart," he said, pulling Andrew closer to him. "Real big."

They sat still and silent, looking down the mountain, Thomas soaking in a rare moment of solitude with his son. He felt gratitude, though it was mixed with sorrow for how rare an occasion like this actually was. He vowed to change that. "How about we head back down to the village?" Thomas asked.

Andrew looked around one last time, then nodded. "Sounds good."

Thomas picked up the backpack and guided them toward the familiar path he would usually take home after meeting with Sophia.

"Good-bye, Sophia!" Andrew shouted.

"I don't think she can hear you, Andrew," Thomas laughed.

"Maybe. But just in case she can." Andrew repeated, "Good-bye, Sophia!"

Thomas smiled and also shouted, "Thanks, Sophia!" Sophia's absence had been a strange gift, but sometimes gifts show up in ways we would never have planned.

TWENTY-ONE

Thomas and Andrew made it back to the village before lunch. They stopped at home so Andrew could change his clothes and pick up his books for school. When they opened the front door, Lena ran from the kitchen to meet them.

"Oh, thank God you're still in one piece," she said, grabbing Andrew and hugging him tightly.

"It was so great! We saw so many things that were really pretty and we hiked a lot and we got lost and we talked and we saw the village from up top and we prayed and…I have to change my clothes." Andrew ran off to his room.

Lena looked at Thomas and crossed her arms.

"Andrew was right. It was great," Thomas said.

"You got lost?"

"Not really," Thomas said.

"Not really?" she asked, a small smile on her lips.

"Well, there was this one point," Thomas whispered, "where

I wanted to make it really exciting for Andrew and I pretended that we were lost."

"Pretended?" Lena asked.

Thomas' only response was his grin.

Andrew ran back and announced, "I better get to school." He started toward the door then turned back to Thomas for a hug.

"Thanks for today, Dad."

"I love you, Andrew. I had a great time."

"See you later, Mom!" Andrew called as the door closed behind him.

"No hug for me? What am I? Just the woman who cooks the food around here?" Lena said, shaking her head. "Maybe he's just so excited about telling everyone at school about what a great father he has and how he took him up on the mountain."

"Most likely," Thomas replied, hoping he was being funny.

"To be honest, I wish he would've come home and wanted me with you guys on the mountain..."

Thomas leaned toward her and lifted her arms, placing them around his waist. "How about a little coffee before I go to work?"

She pulled her arms back, turned, and walked away. "Not today. I have a lot to do."

Thomas was unsure what had just happened. He looked down at the half-opened backpack sitting near him on the floor, with the flowers Andrew had brought for his mother lying inside the front pocket.

He drank his coffee alone, reviewing the events of the morning before leaving for work. He hoped Lena would come around before too long.

When Thomas arrived at his shop, a note from Jonathan was attached to the shop door, a reminder of the dinner invitation for that evening. "Come hungry," the note stated. Thomas pocketed the note and smiled at the thought of spending an evening with friends.

While he worked on projects, he stopped occasionally to reflect on his morning with Andrew. He couldn't help but talk out loud with God. "Thanks for the great time with my son. Thank you for continuing to point out to me how it's possible to see things differently. Please be with Lena today, please make Anna get stronger, give Erik joy, and give Andrew wisdom. I hope he will see you differently after today."

Fascinated by the changes in his life, Thomas considered the day's new lesson. Straying from a familiar path can lead to something beautiful. And sometimes, not getting what you want can be better than anything you dreamed of. Thomas had not gotten what he wanted this morning when Sophia didn't show up, and when he realized he didn't care, he threw his head back and laughed.

TWENTY-TWO

D ad!" Erik screamed as he ran into his father's shop that afternoon.

Thomas wiped his hands on his work apron and threw his arms around his crying son. "What happened, Erik?"

"Andrew is getting killed on the schoolyard!"

Thomas ran out of the shop and, following Erik, ran down Main Street. Andrew walked toward them, his nose bleeding. He had used his shirtsleeve to stop the blood, and the blood was smeared across his cheek.

"Andrew!" Erik cried out.

Thomas grabbed his son and held him close. "What happened?"

Andrew began crying. "Oh, Dad. It was so bad."

Erik looked down at the ground, frowning. "They said we are a crazy mountain-climbing family."

"Is that true?" Thomas asked Andrew.

"Yes," Andrew softly answered. Erik nodded in agreement.

"Let's get back into the shop, get you cleaned up, and then you can tell me everything that happened."

At the shop, Thomas cleaned Andrew's face and got him a drink of cold water. Once Andrew had calmed down, Thomas asked him for details.

"When I got to school today, some of the boys were whispering and making fun of me. One kid said, 'How's your crazy dad?' and everybody laughed. I wanted to say something and all I could think of was, 'You should just be…quiet.' I sounded so stupid."

Erik jumped in. "And one boy said, 'Ooh, I'm so scared.'"

"Didn't your teacher say anything?" Thomas asked.

"Yes," Andrew said. "She said, 'Can someone tell me what's going on here?' and nobody said anything, so she just kept teaching stupid math stuff."

"So when school was out, we walked out onto the playground, and there were all these boys standing there," Erik explained.

Andrew nodded. "One guy said, 'Hey, Andrew, how's the mountain man?' and everyone laughed. I pretended I didn't hear him and kept walking. And then another guy said, 'Where do you think you're going?' and I said, 'I'm going home to be with my family.'"

"I was really scared," Erik added.

"Then somebody yelled out, 'The crazy mountain-climbing family!' And Dad, I'm sorry, but I just got really mad at them. I didn't know what to do or say."

"I understand, son. You sound very brave."

"I said, 'Crazy is being afraid of what you don't know!'"

"That's when they went nuts," Erik said.

"And then I told them that I went with you up the mountain and saw amazing things, and how we could look down on the village and see how small everything was. That's when they all started hitting me and piling on top of me."

"He told me to run, so I did," Erik said.

"But, Dad, even though I was on the bottom of the pile, I could tell these guys were causing more damage to each other than they were to me. So I just worked hard to squeeze out from under them and ran away."

"Good for you, son."

"I ran off, but I left my book bag there on the ground."

Thomas hugged his son, getting blood all over his work apron. "Oh, son, I am so sorry. This is all my fault."

"No, it's not," Andrew looked straight into his father's eyes. "They're just afraid of what they don't know. They aren't like us, right?"

Thomas rested one hand on Andrew's shoulder. "Not yet. But I want them to be brave too. One day, maybe we will all be brave."

TWENTY-THREE

Thomas and his sons headed toward home, but he could not stop thinking about the boys at the school who had done this to his son. He was angry with them, but even more, he was angry with their parents. The boys had learned to despise Thomas from their parents. Why did everyone resent him for wanting more out of his life?

Walking hand in hand with Andrew and Erik, Thomas prayed silently. *God, I'm reminded how much I need your help to make sure the things I am teaching my boys are the things you want them to know. Please remove the thoughts and feelings that you do not want me to have. I can't stand to think about angry words slipping out and staining my sons with hatred and spite.*

Thomas looked down at Andrew's face and saw a drop of blood running from his forehead down his cheek. He hadn't realized there was a cut on his scalp too. Poor kid. He pictured his son earlier that day, running through the field of wild daisies. *He was so happy*, Thomas thought.

Erik looked up at Thomas and asked, "Daddy?"

"Yes?"

"Are you going to ask which boys did this to Andrew and go beat up their dads?"

Thomas smiled. "I'm not sure what I'm going to do."

"You don't have to do anything, Dad," Andrew replied.

"Yeah, Dad," Erik added, trying to be mature like his big brother. "You don't have to do nothing."

Thomas smiled and thought, *Sometimes the voice of God is heard clearest through the voice of a child.*

As they continued walking, Thomas squeezed the hands of his boys a little tighter. Oddly enough, they were not in any hurry to get home. They were together, the men of the family, boldly walking down the middle of Main Street. Thomas cherished the moment, knowing his boys felt completely safe by his side. Terrible things happened in this world, but there was power in walking alongside your father. The touch of his hand made his little ones brave.

Arriving at home, Thomas opened the front door and called out, "Lena?" She came out of the kitchen, wiping her hands on her apron, and saw Thomas and the boys in the front hallway.

"Oh, my God in heaven," she cried as she saw Andrew's face. His right eye was beginning to turn black, and the trickle of blood from the cut on his scalp had left a red trail down his other cheek.

"He's okay," Thomas quickly said.

"He most certainly is not," Lena answered, moving Andrew into the kitchen where she could clean his wounds. "What happened?"

Anna, reclining in her wheelchair next to the table, whispered, "What…?"

"Oh, it was nothing," Andrew shrugged.

Erik quickly jumped in, "Some boys beat up Andrew. I ran away really fast."

Lena cleaned off Andrew's face with a wet cloth, paying close attention to the cut on his scalp.

Andrew continued, "There were just some boys at school…"

"Yes?" Lena urged him to say more.

"And they were making fun of me for climbing the mountain, telling me I was crazy."

She looked him in the eyes. "You are no such thing." She set down the washcloth and hugged him tightly.

"I know." Andrew tried to wiggle out of his mother's tight grasp.

"Are you hurt anywhere else?" Lena asked.

"I'm fine," Andrew answered, pulling away and retreating to his bedroom, Erik close behind.

"He's just like his father," Lena said.

"What do you mean?"

"Stubborn."

"What are you talking about?"

"He doesn't need any help."

"He doesn't need *your* help," Thomas replied.

"Thomas," Lena gasped.

"The boy is growing up," Thomas said. "You and I aren't always going to be there for him when he falls and scrapes his knee. And as much as you might want to run and help him, Lena, you have got to let him get up on his own—just so he knows he can do it by himself."

"But, Thomas, the child was just beaten up by a group of boys!"

"He's all right," Thomas said.

"What are you going to do about this?" Lena asked.

"That...I do not know," Thomas replied and walked out of the kitchen. He had an idea, but he wanted to wait and talk with Jonathan about it that evening after their dinner together.

"You better do something." Lena declared. "This wouldn't have happened if you hadn't climbed that mountain."

Thomas turned around and stared at Lena. "I'm doing this for Anna."

"For...me?" Anna whispered.

"Yes, princess," he said as he leaned down to Anna. "You asked me to climb the mountain. And what I've found is that there's a whole other way of doing life than I have ever imagined. No matter what other people might think, life doesn't have to be the way it has always been. Everyone's life can be full of meaning and significance, even if we don't get everything we want."

Thomas stood and faced Lena. "Doing everything the same way, year after year, has only worn ruts deep into the soil of this village. I don't want to settle for that any longer." He took a deep breath. "If rising above the crowd means simply climbing out of the rut, that's what I am going to do. No matter what other people think. Because what I've learned today is that my life isn't my own. I climbed that mountain thinking I had to save Anna, but I've realized that we all need saving."

Lena was silent.

"I am climbing out of the rut," Thomas said, "and I want you to come with me. Will you?"

"I can't answer that right now," Lena replied softly, turning and exiting the kitchen.

"Please?" Thomas called out. There was no answer. He looked at his ring and prayed, *God, if you are here with me, I certainly don't feel it.*

"Daddy...don't be sad," Anna said. "I'll...go with you."

TWENTY-FOUR

Thomas was changing his clothes as Lena stepped into the bedroom and asked, "When were you going to tell me about our dinner tonight?"

"I thought I told you about it on…" Thomas said.

"Thankfully, I ran into Brigitta at the market today and she filled me in on our plans."

"I am so sorry," Thomas apologized.

"I am sorry too," Lena said and walked out of their bedroom.

"Lena," Thomas followed her out. "Can we go and just have a good time tonight?"

"I guess we have to."

Thomas paused outside their bedroom door, and Lena continued walking toward the kitchen. He shook his head.

"You ready to go, Anna?" Thomas asked his daughter from the hallway.

"Yes…" she answered. Anna hadn't had much of an appetite lately, but she still wanted to be included in the family activities.

"Boys? Are you just about ready?"

"Yes, Dad," Erik answered.

"Andrew?"

"Yes, sir," came the faint reply.

"Are you okay?" Thomas said.

"Yes, Dad. I'm okay."

Thomas cracked open the boys' bedroom door and stuck his head around the edge, "Andrew, I'm very proud of you."

"Thanks, Dad. I'm proud of you too."

"Me too, Andrew," Erik said boldly. "I'm proud of you too."

"Thanks a lot," Andrew said to Erik.

"Let's go, then," Thomas said.

The family walked together, with Erik pushing little Anna in her wheelchair, down the street to Jonathan and Brigitta's. Dinner was potatoes and meatballs, a favorite in Thomas' family.

After everyone had finished eating, Andrew and Erik found their favorite card game and were content playing in the living room while Anna stayed near. The adults stayed at the table discussing what happened on the schoolyard with Andrew. Brigitta and Jonathan thought the bullies should be punished for what they did. Lena agreed.

"But we don't know who they were," Thomas added. "Andrew and Erik don't want to tell."

Brigitta and Lena collected the dirty dishes and carried them into the kitchen together.

"Sounds like the boys are afraid of something happening again," Jonathan said.

The women returned to the dining area just as Jonathan and Thomas were getting up from the table.

"Going somewhere?" asked Lena.

"Jonathan and I are going to take a little walk," Thomas said.

Jonathan moved to Brigitta and kissed her, saying, "Thank

you for dinner. It was wonderful. We will be back soon." The men went out the front door while the women continued to clean up after the evening's meal.

Thomas and Jonathan sat on a bench in the front yard and stared up at the star-filled sky.

Jonathan spoke the first words. "It sure is beautiful."

"Yes," Thomas answered slowly.

"Your boys sure are getting big. And how's Anna doing?" Jonathan said after a while.

"She is not doing well. And it's killing me."

"I'm so sorry, Thomas. Is there anything I can do?"

"I honestly have no idea."

"I'm here if you need anything, anytime. You know that, right, Thomas?"

"I do, Jonathan. Thank you," Thomas answered. "Can I tell you a secret?"

"We've been friends a long time, Thomas."

"Remember Benjamin?"

"Of course I do. That was horrible."

"Yes, it was. And I watched it happen."

"What do you mean?"

"I stood there on the edge of the lake and watched Benjamin fall through the ice. And I just stood there. I couldn't save him. My best friend died, and I couldn't do a thing to stop it. And I feel like, in a lot of ways, I've been stuck on the shore of that frozen lake for the past twenty years. The guilt, the shame, the wondering if there's something I could've done—it's haunted me my whole life."

Jonathan put his hand on Thomas' shoulder.

"And so now with Anna being sick...I'm feeling so helpless. There's got to be something I can do to save her. I can't go back and save Benjamin, but maybe I can save her..."

"How do you think you can save her?"

"That's where it gets weird. I heard Anna tell me to climb the mountain." He pointed to the peak, "Yep, that one right there. So I did, thinking maybe she knew something I didn't. And what I've discovered is something bigger than you and me and Anna and her sickness. I don't know if climbing the mountain is going to heal Anna, but it's given me something I never would've received otherwise. I am thinking about God for the first time in my life."

"This is about God?" Jonathan sounded surprised.

"I think it is," Thomas explained. "At first, this was about Anna, and I still hope that we can find something to help her get better. But what I have found is that God wants to have a personal relationship with me, with you, with everyone. It's like he's calling me off that shore, and as I'm learning more and more about what that means, my life is changing. My egotistical, self-centered ways of thinking about everything are being replaced by thoughts of love and compassion for my family and everyone around me. It's strange, right?"

Jonathan smiled.

"That's all I want to do now," Thomas continued. "I want to keep seeking after what God has, even if it's not what I want for myself."

"Do you think God wants to heal Anna?" Jonathan asked.

"I want to believe he does. But I don't know if God sees things with the same perspective that we have."

"Why would a loving God want a child to suffer?"

"I don't know, Jonathan. I don't think he does. I think God wants everything and everyone to be perfect like it was in the beginning. But it's not. So he's in the process of making things new. That's where I think hope comes in, trusting that God is in the middle of this mess, making something good out of it."

"Even if it doesn't look good to us?" Jonathan wondered.

"Exactly."

Jonathan released a huge sigh and looked up at the stars. "Thomas, I don't completely understand what you're talking about, but I'd like to."

Thomas smiled. "Thank you, friend." Patting his friend on the back, he added, "Jonathan, you are, without question, nice."

Jonathan laughed.

"Do you think you need to do something about the boys in the schoolyard?" Jonathan asked a few moments later.

"I want to," Thomas said, "but I'm not sure what I should do. As it is, I'm not the most liked person in town."

"It's probably more important for you to stand up for what you believe," Jonathan said, "than it is for you to be liked."

Thomas was surprised Jonathan encouraged him to take a risk. "Where did that come from?" he asked.

"You're passionate about what you believe. If you really think what you have to say will be helpful to the rest of the village, I highly recommend saying it."

"You mean that?"

"Absolutely. But don't do something just to make yourself feel better, or to prove to others how you know things that no one else does. That's ignorance."

Thomas thought about Jonathan's words. His anger and frustration over his sons' situation turned into nervous anticipation. He also thought about how angry Lena was at him for getting his son hurt. But deep down he knew she also didn't want to be trapped in the ruts of life either.

"I'm a little scared," Thomas admitted.

"It's good to be a little scared," Jonathan replied.

"Then what are you doing Sunday?"

"Church," Jonathan replied.

"Good. I'm going to need your help."

"Okay, Thomas. But no fighting or setting the church on fire."

Thomas laughed. "I'll have to come up with something else then."

TWENTY-FIVE

Thomas hoped she would be there even though today was Saturday. Sophia had never said anything to Thomas about not meeting on the weekends. He was anxious to talk to her about what had happened the day before, and to find out why she wasn't there to meet him and Andrew.

Thomas and Lena had not spoken to each other when they arrived home from dinner last night. She was angry about what had happened to Andrew, saying it was Thomas' fault. Still, he bent over and kissed her on the cheek as he was leaving this morning.

"I love you, Lena. And I am sorry," he whispered into her ear. She did not stir, but he wasn't sure if she was asleep or just ignoring him.

Thomas was overcome with relief when he arrived and saw Sophia praying on her knees. The sight of her made Thomas feel comforted, as if he had just run home to his mother after a hard day at school. She reminded him so much of his mother that he could almost smell a fresh apple pie baking somewhere nearby.

Sophia looked up and her eyes met his, a soft smile on her face.

"Sophia!" Thomas cried out with joy as he walked toward her.

"Hello, my dear boy," she replied quietly, sounding out each word as if with great care.

It seemed difficult for her to talk, and she moved slowly, as if each turn of her head or arm caused pain. Her condition was strangely similar to Anna's.

"Are you all right?" Thomas asked with concern, moving to her side. She put her finger up to her mouth.

"Today...we use few words," she said. Her giant, radiant smile was still there, but Thomas could see the pain in her eyes.

His thoughts began racing. "But there is so much I need to tell you, and so much I need you to tell me."

Sophia reached for Thomas' hand and placed it over his own heart. He could feel it beating rapidly. He was frightened, and she knew it.

"You want me to listen to my heart? Is that what you want, Sophia? But I have been, and it's only gotten me into a lot of trouble."

"Thomas, life...is very short," she said.

"Yes, Sophia. I know that." Thomas thought of Anna and sighed.

"More than anything...I want you to be convinced...of how much God loves you."

"Sophia, what does God's love matter when bad things happen? Like Anna being so sick. If he loved me, or her, wouldn't she get better?"

"It matters..." She paused to catch her breath, and then finished her thought. "Everything."

"But, Sophia…"

"Even when you do not feel it, or it does not seem like it is enough for what you are going through…it is all you need." Sophia's voice became more and more quiet, her eyes slowly closed, and her head lowered to her chest. Thomas wanted to reach for her and hold her upright, but he was afraid.

"What about Anna? What about my daughter?"

Sophia lifted her head and spoke. "Her pain, her sickness, her disease…she is being made new."

"What do you mean?"

"God sent me here, Thomas, to meet with you. To help you know love. To help you know a hope that keeps your eyes turned toward the mountain, even when everything tries to pull your gaze to the ground."

"You're an angel?"

"A messenger. As we grow in our relationship with God, he uses us to spread messages of hope."

"And now that I've done your assignments, you…and God… are going to heal my daughter, right? That's why I've been coming here."

"Healing comes in many ways."

"That's not what I want to hear, Sophia. Tell me my daughter's going to be okay."

"What seems good in our eyes…isn't always the same…as good in God's eyes."

"Sophia." He placed his hand on her arm.

She looked at Thomas with intensity. "No matter what happens, Thomas…love…him…back."

Sophia eased herself back down to a kneeling position for prayer. "Please, go…" she whispered. "I will see you again." She took a deep breath and pointed to the path. "Leave now. Do not waste this time. It is a gift."

TWENTY-SIX

Thomas staggered down the mountain, lost in his confusion. Sophia's words replayed in his mind over and over again. Thomas felt so hopeless about Anna, and how to awaken the slumbering souls in the village below, and even how to love God.

"Is that what you want?" he prayed aloud. "You want me to feel helpless and not able to do anything?"

He heard an answer. It wasn't an actual voice, like some people might have expected, but rather, it was as if the answer was whispered in his ear, or as if he felt the words in his heart.

On your own, you are helpless, the voice said. *Now that you realize this, I can finally use you.*

"Use me?" Thomas answered.

The things you want to do in your life, I also want to do, but in a deeper, more significant way than you can even imagine.

"How will you do that?"

Trust me.

"But what am I supposed to do?" Thomas said.

Trust me.

Thomas did not think trusting God was a practical way to accomplish anything. "Yes, but I can do so much more than that," he began. "Just tell me what you want me to do."

Trust me.

Thinking of Anna, Thomas fell to his knees in humility. The only thing Thomas truly wanted was beyond his abilities.

"God, please forgive me," he cried out, "for thinking I have anything else to give. All I have is from you. And anything I want to accomplish in my life can only be done by you. If loving you means trusting you, then that is what I will do." Thomas paused as he thought about what awaited him at home. He lifted his face up to the soft blue sky as clouds slowly rolled past.

"But, God, the only reason I climbed that mountain was for Anna. I know now that you wanted to change me and make me the man you created me to be, but what about her? When does she get her answer to prayer?" Thomas raised his voice. "Why don't you seem to care?"

She's my daughter too. And yes, you can trust me, even with Anna. I will never let her leave my sight.

Thomas' words to Lena from a few days ago returned to him, and Thomas hung his head, then nodded. Trust might be the hardest thing he had ever done.

TWENTY-SEVEN

The family was eating breakfast in the kitchen, with Anna sitting up. She smiled broadly when Thomas walked into the room, a spark in her eyes that he hadn't seen for months. Perhaps it was because Lena had made her famous heart-shaped buttermilk waffles that Anna loved, with cardamom as the secret ingredient, served with a choice of goat cheese and fresh lingonberries. Lena always cooked with love—with love for her family and with love for the food. She had a way of combining simple ingredients into something that fed not only their stomachs but their hearts too.

"Dad, did you meet Sophia?" Erik asked.

"Yes, I did," Thomas replied, looking at Anna. "How are you doing today, princess?"

"These are the best waffles!" Anna said.

Thomas looked at Lena with surprise.

"Anna woke up with a new level of energy, and the first thing she said was, 'How about some waffles this morning?' How could I refuse?"

"And I can't refuse to eat them," Andrew said. "They are so good. More please."

"There's plenty for all my favorite children."

"And their father, hopefully," Thomas added.

"Yes, dear. Even you."

Breakfast was the beginning of a great family day together. Lena made a picnic for lunch out by the lake. Anna and her mother stayed on a blanket most of the time, while Thomas and the boys threw a ball around. Anna laughed at her brothers' antics, and the boys hammed it up for their sister.

That evening, as they lay next to each other in bed, Thomas reached out to hold Lena's hand. They had spent a good day together as a family, but he knew Lena was still holding on to some pain about what had happened to Andrew.

"Honey, we have to get on the same page about how we're going to live our lives."

"I completely agree," Lena responded.

"Is this all about deciding whether we're going to let other people determine how we live our lives, or are we, with God's help, going to live the lives we want to live?"

"I think it's more complicated than that."

"What do you mean?" Thomas asked, propping himself up on his side.

"If living our own lives means that our children will get hurt, then we can't do that. But if living for other people means that we stay trapped inside a prison of unrealistic expectations, then we can't do that either. Where's the middle ground?"

"I think the middle ground, if that's what we're going to call it, is found by seeking God, and by trusting that he loves us, no matter what happens to us. And then trying to love the people around us."

"That sounds beautiful, Thomas. I'm just not sure how to actually do that," Lena said.

"I'm not either. But I do know that I'm going to need your help."

Lena didn't say anything, but she squeezed Thomas' hand. He leaned down to kiss her on the cheek, and then laid next to her in the silence. Softly, they heard Anna singing in the night's calm. She sang an old hymn that she had learned as a child, and as Thomas drifted to sleep, he let the sound of his daughter's faith comfort him.

Twenty-Eight

Sunday came to Bergland, and the villagers found their way into the church sanctuary for the morning service. Thomas and his family sat in their usual seats in the fourth row from the front, left side. Gunnar Tollefsrud, who had been playing the same few songs over and over for most of his eighty years, was in his place in front of the organ. The congregation sat down after the opening hymn, and one of the elders began reading the Scripture passage of the day.

Thomas was having difficulty paying attention. He was busy looking around at the different families with young boys, wondering which ones had beat up Andrew. He would see a boy who looked liked he was Andrew's age, try to make out any black eyes or bruises, and then see the boy's father. He wished Andrew had told him who the boys were.

Lena cleared her throat. Thomas looked at her, and she signaled for him to focus on what was being said from the pulpit. It was just like he was twelve years old again with his own mother scolding him in church.

Pastor Sundquist began the week's sermon on hell by talking about people in this world who were not the least bit afraid of spending eternity in a pit of fire.

"How can this be?" the pastor asked. "It's simple. People get used to the smell of smoke. They get used to the heat of the fire."

Thomas chewed his bottom lip, thinking of what he was about to do.

"Too many people have been playing with fire during their lives here on earth," Pastor Sundquist continued. "They have lost all feeling in their hands and in their hearts. They have forgotten to be afraid."

"Amen," someone in the back of the church shouted.

Thomas turned his head to the right and looked at Lena, who was intently listening to the sermon, and Anna in her wheelchair in the aisle. He saw Jonathan and his wife sitting across the aisle. They caught his gaze, and Thomas gave Jonathan a thumbs-up. Jonathan hesitantly gave a thumbs-up back.

Thomas looked at his boys. Andrew stared up at him. "Pray for me," Thomas whispered as he slipped out of the pew and into the aisle, walking toward the pulpit.

The congregation began whispering to each other.

The pastor stopped mid-sentence as Thomas approached him.

"I'm sorry, Pastor, I will just be a minute," Thomas said.

"Do you think this could wait until I'm finished here?"

Thomas turned to face the congregation. Everyone stared with looks of disbelief and amazement. He noticed several mouths had dropped completely open. People seemed to be holding their breath to see what he was going to do.

"Good morning, everyone," he said solemnly. "I am very

concerned about what is happening between all of us here in the village. You probably know by now that I have been climbing the mountain. Yes, I realize the risk I am taking. I believe it's time for a new perspective on life here in Bergland. We have been doing the same things over and over for far too long. The ruts we have dug for ourselves have hindered our vision from seeing anything outside of our own little village. We have lost sight of hope. We rarely even talk to each other. But we do talk within our homes, and your children have picked up some of the things you have been saying to each other. That is how I found out about your feelings, by seeing what your children did to my son after school on Friday."

The church was deathly silent. Thomas looked around and stared directly into the eyes of anyone who would meet his gaze. A few people appeared interested in what he had to say, but he wondered if he was indeed crazy.

"In the process of trying to discover what the mountain has to offer, I have found that hope is real. That there truly is more to this life than just living day to day, stuck in the daily grind. And that hope is found knowing that God wants to have a personal relationship with me, with all of us."

People began to murmur. A few people shifted uncomfortably in their seats.

"This isn't about church," Thomas said. "This is about getting to know God, letting him get to know us, and allowing him to open our hearts and minds to fill them with hope. Then our lives will have so much more meaning and significance. That's what it really means to climb the mountain."

Someone shouted from the back of the room. "What if we don't want to change?"

A few people chuckled.

Thomas smiled. "That's a good question." He cleared his

throat and looked at Anna sitting in the middle aisle in her wheelchair, watching him with wide eyes.

"Change is difficult," he said. "It stirs things up, makes us uncomfortable at times. I can't blame you if you don't want to change. But if you hear nothing else from me today, please hear this. There is more to this life than many of us are now experiencing. I'm not saying that bad things will stop happening. I don't believe that this relationship with God is necessarily going to heal my daughter, Anna, though we are still hoping for a miracle. But God is God, and I'm not. And what I've found is that this God we talk about here every Sunday brings meaning and significance to everything that happens to us—the good and the bad. He offers us hope, a way of looking at life that sees the value in every situation and every person. Hope anticipates God is working to make all things good. I am only just beginning to understand what all this means. But I'm on my way, and I would love to take anyone with me who would like to go."

He looked around the room and saw people whispering to each other and shaking their heads.

"Can you feel in your heart what I am talking about? Maybe you don't completely understand what I'm talking about, but if you'd like to find out, that is what I'm looking for. Is there anyone here who is willing to go on this journey with me?"

Thomas let a minute of silence pass. Suddenly, Andrew jumped up onto the wooden pew. "I will go with you, Dad."

Erik jumped up on the pew as well. "Me too," he added. Anna echoed her brothers, sitting up taller in her wheelchair.

Lena looked at the kids, and then at her husband. She stood and said, "I will go with you, Thomas."

A woman gasped from across the room.

Jonathan and Brigitta immediately stood up, holding hands. "We will go with you too."

Tears flooded Thomas' eyes. The most important people in his life were standing up with him. Another minute passed and no one else stood.

"Is that it?" Thomas asked.

A man in the back stood up and said sternly, "You can go your own way, Thomas, but the rest of us are going to stick together."

"I am not going my own way," Thomas answered. "I've been doing that my whole life."

The man in the back sat back down. Thomas waited another minute before he started walking down the middle aisle toward the back door. Lena, the kids, and Jonathan and Brigitta followed him down the aisle.

"Have a nice time on the mountain," someone yelled out from the crowd, followed by scattered laughter.

Thomas stopped and turned around. "If you ever change your mind, I would be glad to walk beside you every step of the way."

Together with his friends and family, Thomas continued out the door and into the bright sunlight of the morning.

TWENTY-NINE

Sophia had challenged him to awaken the slumbering souls around him, but Thomas had no idea how difficult that would be. Walking out of the church, with only his family and close friends, Thomas was discouraged and confused. Why didn't more people want to live an awakened life?

He thought of escaping Bergland in search of a village where people were open-minded and the stubborn rules of Janteloven weren't as domineering. He'd be happier if he didn't have to live here.

Love makes you brave.

He turned around and looked to be sure no one had spoken those words. He couldn't believe that God actually whispered to him in his heart. But the words remained, and his family and friends were busy talking about the events in church.

Thomas wondered what it meant to be brave in this situation.

Leaving Bergland seemed like a coward's way of avoiding further pain. Staying would require spiritual bravery, not to mention trust and faith; things Thomas never thought he had until now. But what he received on the mountain was building a foundation in him, enabling him to be brave like never before. It was as if Thomas had placed one foot onto the frozen ice and was ready to leave the shore forever. He wasn't worried about losing his own life. He was worried about watching anyone else lose their life.

Jonathan and Brigitta said their good-byes and went home after a round of hugs.

Arriving at home, Lena prepared a lunch of dark rye bread topped with cheese and pickled fish as well as a fresh cucumber salad.

When they all sat down to eat, little Erik broke the silence first. "Church was fun today."

"It sure was," Thomas answered, rubbing his hand over Erik's head. They laughed together at how dumbfounded Pastor Sundquist was when Thomas went up front.

"Are we going to leave Bergland?" Andrew asked.

Thomas set down his fork. "Why do you ask that, Andrew?"

"I don't know," he answered, "it just seems like people at school don't like me. And then at church today, nobody was very nice to us either."

"I don't want to go…" Anna said, then worked to catch her breath. She had been so strong this weekend, Thomas thought. Yesterday had been like a gift.

Chills ran along Thomas' spine. This weekend was a gift. Somehow, in a way Thomas could not humanly understand, God had allowed Sophia to give them this time. He focused again on Anna and thought about her comment.

"I don't either, princess. But let me ask you all this question. What do you think it means to be brave in this situation?"

"In my favorite books, the hero always defeats the enemy," Erik said.

"There's not going to be any more fighting in this family," Lena said.

"Anna, do you remember what you told me about the story in your picture book?" Thomas asked.

"About the prince?" she replied, her breath coming more slowly now.

"Yes. Anna, why was the prince brave when he was rescuing the princess?"

"Because...of love," Anna answered.

"Yes, because of love. I think for us to be brave we have to stay and love these people, no matter what they say about us or do to us."

"That sounds hard," Andrew said. He reached up and touched the cut on his scalp, as if reminding himself of the pain.

"I think it will be, son. But I have great hope that love is the very thing this village needs. Even if it starts just with us, it has to start. What do you think?"

Thomas looked at Lena and at each of the kids, who looked back at their father with wide-eyed wonder.

"More than anything, I want my life to be fueled by my love for you all," Thomas continued. "I want my life to be grounded in faith in God. I want to listen and look for him in all situations. I believe that we are in his hands right now, and that he is holding on to us and caring for us better than we can imagine. But I also want to be guided by vision for the future, for how great life can be, mostly because of the greatness of God. This love, this faith, this vision, all working together to create hope—this is how I want to live. This is how I believe we can all live."

"So you're asking us to hang on to God, no matter what?" Lena asked.

"I believe we have to," Thomas replied.

"I can do that, Dad," Andrew said.

"Me too," Erik piped in.

"Always...hope," Anna said with a smile.

"No matter what," Lena added.

After lunch, the family took blankets to the lake and sprawled out in the sunshine, spending the day reading, resting, and playing. Spring was in full bloom, and the birds were singing their happy, hopeful tunes. Andrew lifted Anna onto his back and carried her around to see every variety of flower they could find, Erik leading the way.

That evening, Thomas gathered the family together into a circle on the floor of the living room. "I want to say thank you to each of you for going on this journey of hope with me," Thomas began, his face glowing in the light of several candles he had lit. He smiled at Lena. "I know this has been a confusing time for all of us. But I have incredible hope that, starting today, life is going to be better than we could have ever imagined. And no matter what, we will always be a family, with God watching over us."

"Yes," Anna said.

"When do we get to see God?" Erik asked innocently. Andrew punched him on the shoulder.

Thomas grinned. "I believe we will see him in many unexpected ways." He reached out his hand to Lena on his left and Andrew on his right. Andrew took Erik by the hand, and Erik and Lena both held Anna's hands.

"But until then, Erik, let's keep talking to him."

For the first time as a family, they each took turns praying to God. When they finished, they all sat quietly together, still holding hands in the glow of the candlelight.

Anna looked tired as Thomas tucked her into bed that evening. The difficulty breathing and fever seemed to be coming back. Thomas wondered if maybe they had done too much, played too hard, laughed too loud.

"My princess, my beautiful little princess. You get some good rest tonight, okay?"

"I will…Daddy," Anna said as Thomas pulled the covers up over her body and placed the cool washcloth on her forehead. "Oh…" Anna opened her eyes, as if she was remembering something. "Tell Sophia…thank you."

"Thank you? For what, honey?"

"For making…you not sad…" Anna said.

"What? What are you talking about?" Thomas couldn't imagine that Anna would be making this up.

"In the hospital, I saw…it was her. I said…I didn't…want you…to be sad."

"Oh, Anna." Thomas lay down in the bed next to his daughter.

"She said…I have a gift…to see…what's important…" Anna was struggling to breathe.

"Take your time, Anna. It's okay." Thomas held his daughter in his arms.

She caught her breath and said, "And if I need help…look up. She said…hope is there…" Anna said, pointing out her window toward the mountain.

"Anna, I love you so much," Thomas said quietly. "You have no idea what you've done for me. You've helped me to see things better, more clearly. To see what matters."

Tears filled Anna's eyes as she smiled. Her breathing settled as she slowly fell asleep in her father's arms.

THIRTY

Anna never woke up the next morning.

The family gathered at her bedside, taking turns holding her hand and stroking her hair. By the time the doctor arrived, Erik was sobbing, sitting close to his mother while she wept. Thomas held Andrew, who struggled to find any words at all. They played Anna's favorite album, Edvard Grieg's *Norwegian Dances*. As a toddler, Anna had danced around the living room while the happy songs had played.

The doctor waited in the living room while they said their final good-byes.

"Does anybody want to say anything?" Thomas asked.

Andrew wiped his sniffles and stood up. "I do."

Thomas was shocked but did not stop him. "Anything you want, son."

He looked at his sister lying so still and started to cry again.

"It's okay, Andrew. There's no rush," Thomas said.

"Anna, you are so beautiful. And now you're all better. I'm

so…happy for you." He couldn't continue through the tears and sat back down. Thomas held him tight.

"Can I say something?" Erik asked.

"Of course you can, Erik," Lena responded.

Erik stood up and tried to put on his brave face. "Anna, I love you. And you'll always be my sister. I'll never forget you. And I'll see you in heaven. Will you save me a seat next to you? Thank you. Amen."

Thomas and Lena smiled through their tears.

"Lena?" Thomas looked at his wife.

"Oh my precious, little Anna," Lena began, still holding Erik. "You were an answer to our prayers in the beginning, and you always will be. There will never be a day that goes by when I won't think about you and wish you were here, with your smile and your laughter."

Thomas cleared his throat and wiped his eyes. "Erik, Andrew, Lena, and Anna, we are a family. And while good and bad things will continue to happen to us, we will never stop being family— nothing will ever change that. I am so happy we have each other. I am so thankful for Anna's life. She taught us how to hang on to joy, even in the midst of great suffering. We will never be the same. Thank you, Anna. And thank you, God, for Anna. Help us to love each other even more now."

The doctor eased into the room, nodding at Thomas. Thomas stood and led his family into the kitchen while the doctor confirmed that Anna was gone and then called the undertaker. Thomas watched it all unfold as if in a dream.

He sat and cried with his family, everyone holding each other tightly, while Anna's music played on.

They buried Anna the following evening at sunset. While

everyone in town knew that Anna had died, only Jonathan, Brigitta, and Pastor Sundquist showed up for the graveside service.

"I am sorry for your loss," Pastor Sundquist offered.

"Thank you, Pastor," Thomas said.

"I've been thinking about the message you spoke on Sunday," he whispered to Thomas. "I wish I had your bravery."

Thomas smiled.

The pastor opened the Bible and began.

"'O Death, where is your sting? O Hades, where is your victory?' The sting of death is sin, and the strength of sin is the law. But thanks be to God, who gives us the victory through our Lord Jesus Christ."

Pastor Sundquist stopped and looked up. "I'll stop for now, as I'm sure Thomas has plenty he'd like to say."

Thomas took the pastor's place in front of the mostly empty chairs that had been set up next to Anna's grave. He saw Lena's eyes widen as she noticed that he was wearing his father's belt for the very first time. He nodded to her in response. He felt ready to wear it now.

Thomas began reading from his notes. "As we lay our precious Anna into the ground, we watch the sun disappear behind the mountain. But tomorrow will arrive soon, and with it a new sunrise and another day to love those around us."

He paused and looked around at the other gravestones, and then at each person sitting before him. Lena and Erik were both crying. Andrew was trying hard to hold back his tears.

"Do you mind if I don't read my notes?" Thomas asked. "It doesn't seem right."

Jonathan smiled as Thomas folded up the paper and placed it in his coat pocket.

"Here we are. We all knew this day was coming, didn't we? But yet we tried with all our might to believe it wasn't. We held on to what we have called hope—hope that Anna would somehow miraculously get better. She did. What a great weekend we had together. It was like she knew the end was near and just wanted it to be a happy ending instead of a sad one. Somehow, she was given the strength to live, really live, for a few more hours."

Isaac and his wife arrived at the cemetery. Thomas acknowledged them with a nod and a smile.

"But honestly," Thomas said, "I don't know if what we were holding on to was actually hope. To me, the great hope I want to carry with me is that I am deeply loved by God, my creator. And that you are deeply loved by God as well. That we each have incredible value and purpose in this world. And that God is with us in the midst of whatever it is we are going through, whether it's a disease like Anna had, or whether it's the grief we are all feeling right now. God is somehow in this, and he is turning us into the men and women that we are supposed to be. Hope is hanging on to that truth, no matter the circumstances."

Two more families from the village suddenly arrived at the cemetery, taking up a half dozen more of the empty seats. Thomas smiled at Lena.

"To say that Anna's death was meaningless," Thomas continued, "would be to rob her life of the incredible beauty it had. Her life was indeed a gift, but one that required her to give everything else away. But the gift was to me, and I believe, to all of us. We can no longer just go through the motions of life. Her death is a wake-up call to us. The pain, this sadness, is building in us compassion so we can care for one another."

More people began showing up at the gravesite. Each person's arrival was a sign to him that perhaps the town was willing to accept his message of hope.

"I'm so thankful to all of you for coming. I look forward to seeing what's ahead for us here in Bergland. I know that God is at work, taking our joy and our pain, and somehow working all of it together to make something beautiful. Our fear has kept us apart. Now, let Anna's life and her great love bring us together."

Several people said "amen" in response. Andrew's hand shot into the air, causing a few in attendance to smile.

"Yes, my son?"

"Dad, can I say a prayer?" he asked.

"Of course you can. Come up here."

Andrew stood next to his dad, who placed his arm around his son.

"God, I just want to say thank you for my sister. And for my brother and my mom and my dad. I don't understand why people have to die. But I know that you'll take care of her real good. And, God, I pray that you'll help all of us who are still here to get along with each other. Cause we're all we got."

"Amen," Thomas announced. The rest of the crowd that had gathered joined in with a hearty "amen" as well. Thomas hugged his son.

After the service, one of the men came over to Thomas and whispered in his ear. "Thank you for what you said in church. Your daughter must have been so proud of you that day." He walked off to join his wife, and Thomas smiled to himself. Change wasn't easy, but life was too precious not to risk it.

A short time later, another man approached Thomas. "I am very sorry for your loss. And thank you for finally saying what I have been thinking all along. You are a brave man."

Thomas placed his hand on the man's arm. "Love makes us brave."

The man's eyes widened in disbelief. "But what you did, urging us all to live without fear, and with hope, knowing that you were going to lose your daughter?"

Grief stabbed Thomas, but he looked the villager in the eyes.

"I did not lose her. That's exactly why I can live without fear. That is the reason for hope."

Tears filled the man's eyes and he walked quietly away, unable to speak.

Before they left the cemetery, nearly a dozen men and women came to Thomas to offer their condolences and express their appreciation for what he had done at church. Families began to share their own stories of loss, and Thomas did what he could to comfort and encourage them too.

When the family arrived home, they discovered several baskets of food and many more sympathy cards left at their front door.

"I think we're going to be okay here," Lena said, brushing tears from her cheek as she walked in the house.

"I think so too." Thomas replied.

THIRTY-ONE

The next morning, while still in bed, Thomas noticed the sun had begun to rise, and he knew he had to go meet Sophia. "I'll return soon," he promised Lena, kissing her forehead, and he jogged down the road toward the mountain.

He was running with greater strength than he had felt in years. Did Sophia already know of Anna's death? Did she understand the changes taking place in the village? Thomas' world had been turned upside down, and yet the peace he felt about the future was inexplicable. This surely was a miracle.

He arrived at their meeting place, but she was nowhere to be found. "Sophia! Where are you? Sophia!" His voice echoed off the mountain wall.

As his words died out, he heard music floating through the air. It was Sophia's singing. He ran down the path she usually walked, only to find the path ended a short way past the secret place. There was nowhere for him to go, and the music faded.

Thomas returned to the clearing and sat down. The quiet

was overwhelming. Only a gentle breeze moved through the nearby bushes. Loneliness began to replace the strength that had carried him up the path this morning. *Is my new hope really this fragile?* he wondered.

The sun inched its way up the horizon and revealed a clear view of the village, as a gleam of sunlight burst through the bushes in front of Thomas. Following the light into the shadows just behind him, he found a small silver box hidden in the cleft of the rock, sparkling in the light.

He quickly removed the string around the box and took off the lid. Inside were a letter and a bag of seeds.

Thomas,

It has become clear to me that our heavenly Father would desire me to be with him at this time. My time with you is done, for now. I am returning to my place on the other side of the mountain for my final days. My first thought is one of regret at never being able to see you again, but that thought is quickly erased by the thought of seeing my Savior face to face. We only see through a glass dimly while here on earth. But these last few days have been a time of cleansing, polishing, and refining. The glass has become so clear that I can see our Lord as if he is right in front of me, arms reaching out, calling my name. His face is filled with a love that cannot be described.

I am so sorry for the grief you must endure. Yet I know that Anna is with our Lord, and she too has found a new strength. She will never suffer again. I wish that I could have healed her in the way you wanted. Don't think for a moment that I didn't have arguments with God about how he should work.

Now, let God be your comforter and not the one you blame.

Your life will now be an act of worship, meeting with him wherever you are, resting in his love, and sharing it with others.

This bag of seeds I leave for you is a symbol of hope. You have been through a lot over the past several days, and the thing I am most proud of is how your heart has come alive. You've truly been awakened to hope. Now live it out. Use these seeds to demonstrate to others that God can take some dirt and a few small seeds and create something incredibly beautiful.

I will tell our Father how proud I am of you.

Sophia

With tears of joy and sadness, Thomas folded the letter and held it against his chest. He planted a few of the seeds there in their secret place and took the rest with him.

On his way down the mountain, Thomas started dreaming about how Bergland could become new for each of the villagers, perhaps a place where choices were limitless and they could think beyond their small surroundings. A place where people cared about each other and where Janteloven only existed as a distant memory. Maybe his family, together with Jonathan and Brigitte, could help turn Bergland into this sort of place. Anna would be so proud.

And her brothers could start to dream about who they wanted to be. Thomas didn't care so much about what they would do. He wanted to know who they were going to be. That was all that mattered in this new life. They would turn their home into a place that would welcome anybody—it didn't matter what you believed or how you lived, you'd always be invited in to come and be loved. He would create a new garden where he could plant Sophia's seeds, and he would tell people the story of a princess and the mountain.

He couldn't wait to get back down to the village and start rebuilding—not only his house, but the village and his family. Anna had given her life to lead him to this moment, and he would not waste it. Time was a gift.

Just as Thomas hit the village road at the base of the mountain, he saw Lena in the distance, heading toward him.

"Lena!" Thomas called out. They ran to each other, and Lena's faced beamed with love. He could see that she had been crying, and yet the peace he felt was clearly hers as well.

"Jonathan and Brigitta are watching the boys. I want to see this place on the mountain you've been talking about."

Thomas grabbed her and held her tight. He looked into her eyes. "Oh, my love, there is no need to climb the mountain anymore. The secret place can be wherever we make it. Here, come with me."

Her took her hand and walked down the village path to the church, past the pastor's home and into the town cemetery. When they arrived at Anna's grave, something was different.

"Where did that come from?" Lena asked.

Thomas saw the single flower planted in front of their daughter's headstone. It was a daisy, just like the ones Thomas and Andrew had found in the field on the side of the mountain, and it was surely from the same seeds Sophia left for Thomas in the box.

"I can only imagine," he replied. Kneeling down together, they took four seeds out of the bag from Sophia and planted them deep in the soil next to the flower that was already blooming.

Thomas and his family distributed the seeds to the families of Bergland. Now each family had a choice: to let the seeds grow and blossom into something beautiful, or leave the seeds on a shelf without ever having seen the sun. Thomas knew that only time would reveal each family's choice. Some would ignore the invitation to plant a new seed, choosing instead to watch the seeds gather dust over the long years ahead. Others would decide to dig through the cold, dark earth and release the seeds, knowing each would be broken and, with time and God's grace, transformed.

That next spring, Thomas watched as hundreds of new flowers blossomed and the village grew in beauty. He knew Anna was smiling as she watched from her Father's side. Bergland slowly became known throughout the country as a beautiful village filled with endless fields of flowers and the friendliest of families. Soon, people from all over the country visited every spring to witness the incredible beauty of the quaint village.

The irony was not lost on Thomas. He had once longed for escape, but instead God had used him to turn a frozen village into an oasis for others. The boy who could not save his best friend became the man who saved a village.

This, then, was the real miracle they had all needed, the message of hope: that everyone had a choice, not in the events of their lives, but whether they would choose to plant seeds of hope and trust that, one day, beauty would rise.

THANKS

From Mark Smeby

This book was Ceceil Kemp's idea; it wouldn't exist without him. I'm so grateful to him and his wife, Patty. They literally prayed this book into existence. I was also greatly aided by one of my heroes, Anne Lamott, and her *Bird By Bird* book. When I didn't think I could write any more words, she gave me generous handfuls of ideas that would open up vistas of possibilities for my characters. My sister and closest friend, Jody, gave me invaluable assistance throughout the writing process. She was my coach, my editor, and the main reader I had in mind as I wrote. She called me "John Boy"—so I should really thank *The Waltons* and *Little House on the Prairie* while I'm at it, for their influence on us—duh, kinda obvious, right? My parents, Alan and Sharee Smeby, have been amazing encouragers to me all along the journey, reminding me not to give up—that there is indeed something valuable within these pages.

Thanks to my friend and agent Brian Mitchell at Working Title Agency, mostly for being my friend, but also being willing to shop this manuscript around. To Carlton Garborg, David Sluka, and the team at BroadStreet Publishing for breathing life into these embers. And to Ginger Garrett for so many great ideas and challenging me to keep making the book better. If left to myself, this would simply be a "nice" book.

I also want to say thank you to my Grandma Mildred (Smeby). She was a brilliant woman and former English professor. We lived life with very different spiritual paradigms. But I wanted to write this book in such a way that a person like her would hopefully be able to see God a little more clearly than before. She died in May 2010. But I have framed a letter she wrote to me after she read an early draft of this book—perhaps it's similar to something she would have written on one of her student's papers. She wrote:

> Your profound faith is clearly apparent on every page. The descriptions of everyday life of these stolid residents as lived, are alive. Symbolism and metaphors are useful to depict the inner person of these villagers. Humorous touches lighten up philosophical dissertations of a higher life. You are one heck of a writer! Keep it up!
>
> Your appreciative, loving Grandma

I pray you will find someone like Grandma Mildred, or my sister, or my parents, or Sophia—someone who will cheer you on as you keep choosing to take the next steps on your journey.

From Cecil O. Kemp, Jr.

There are a few people I want to thank for their support, encouragement, and contributions along the path to the various iterations of this book.

The path began with Wes Yoder and Ron Miller introducing Mark and me in 2001. I am eternally grateful to Wes and Ron for suggesting the collaboration between Mark and me that has ultimately concluded as *The Messenger*. It has been a match made in heaven.

And on that note, my highest thanks go to my Savior and Lord, Jesus.

Many have prayed for the coming together and going forth of this book. None more vigilant than my prayer warrior wife, Patty. As Mark has noted in his thank-you notes, Patty literally joined me to pray this book into existence. She and our two spiritual mentors, Dora Medaris and Clara Millican, are my Sophias who pointed me to the message of real hope and taught me many of the life, relationship, leadership, and spiritual principles highlighted in *The Messenger*.

Like Mark, I want to thank Brian Mitchell who served as my literary agent and Mark's. He connected us to BroadStreet and its amazing staff of professionals who have made enormous contributions to taking Mark's and my earlier collaborative efforts to the next level. Mark has cited specific BroadStreet staff and others to whom I too want to say thank you so much.

Last but not least, I want to thank Mark who I love, admire, and respect as a man of God and one of the most talented individuals I have ever met. Thank you, Mark, for all your tireless efforts and huge contributions to creating *The Messenger*.

About the Authors

Mark Smeby is a Nashville-based author, speaker, and singer/songwriter who is all about hope—creating products, resources, and live events all focused around the topic. He travels the country sharing the message of hope through his music and speaking engagements—in a variety of locations, such as churches, corporations, schools, and prisons. His one minute daily radio feature, the Live Hope Minute, is heard on radio stations around the country. He has released four CDs (available on iTunes and other digital outlets) and released numerous songs to Christian radio. He costarred in an episode of ABC's hit series *Nashville* and has acted in several faith-based films, including *Gracia, 1 Message, The Perfect Gift,* and *The Hepburn Girls.* Connect with Mark at MarkSmeby.com.

Cecil O. Kemp, Jr. is a life coach, leadership mentor, a sought-after speaker, and author of ten books. A successful CPA, business owner, and executive, Cecil, along with his wife Patty, founded and operate two globally-based entities: The Wisdom Company and The DiffferenceMaker Foundation. Through those entities and their personal efforts, the Kemps encourage and equip individuals to live and lead by Jesus' servant model of living and leadership and thereby leave a positive imprint in every person they are privileged to touch. Married for over four decades, Cecil and Patty are residents of greater Nashville, TN, parents of two adult children, and four times grandparents. To contact Cecil and learn more about him, visit his website: Difference-Maker.net.

For more about *The Messenger*,
including audio book,
companion music CD project,
discussion starters, and more, visit
WWW.MARKSMEBY.COM